A Note From The Author
of Field of Influence

My wounds were more than surface deep; I could hardly breathe. The weight of my consequences pressed me so hard from all sides that I no longer knew which direction was forward. I was captive in a prison of my own making. The chains that bound me cut deeper the harder I tried to free myself from their grip, and the result of this struggle, has scarred me for life. I'm proud to declare that freedom was gained, but this victory didn't come without immense cost. From this war stems my desire to encourage the weary fighter, enlighten the confused bystander, and help birth new beginnings founded on faith.

Before starting this novel, I ask that the reader give a genuine effort towards an open mind. The subject matter revealed is intense, but straight from the core of human struggle. This project is a graphic look inside the depths of a soul. When writing, careful consideration went into every thought and no page was completed without asking the Lord for His approval and blessing. My hope is that all who read this story understand the sovereign nature and perfect love of our almighty God and that nothing is beyond His ability to restore.

Jenny Reese Clark

Jenny Reese Clark

FIELD

OF

INFLUENCE

FIELD
— OF —
INFLUENCE

A Novel by
Jenny Reese Clark

JENNY REESE CLARK
Montgomery, Alabama

Field of Influence
Published by JENNY REESE CLARK
33 Gaylan Court
Montgomery, AL 36109
www.jennyreeseclark.com

ISBN: 978-0-9962440-0-8
Copyright © 2015 by Jenny Reese Clark
Cover design by Eric Abel

Printed in the United States of America 2015

First Edition

10 9 8 7 6 5 4 3 2 1

ACKNOWLEDGEMENTS

Special thanks...

To Marines Josh Mann, Jim Peterson, and Steven Bray who all freely shared in order for this message of hope to be carried on to their brothers.

To the Abel, Reese, and Shoults family who have went above and beyond in love, prayer, and sacrificing their time and talents.

To my friends and the body of believers surrounding me who never stopped praying.

To my technical support Ashley Eiman, Allison H. Williams, and Janie Jones who helped teach me the importance of details.

To my precious Lord and Savior, Jesus Christ, who has held my hand through every page and never ceased to strengthen me.

May we all share equally in the Lord's victory.

To change one's field of influence is to change the course of one's life.

CHAPTER ONE

I have come to a point. If I move one more step in any direction, I have to acknowledge that I passed serious long ago. I pursue an ever-eluding precursor of death, and I'm never satisfied when I find it. The time I spend in pleasure does not outweigh the chase, and the reasons why I continue in this parody of life baffle me.

Although the wheels turn beneath me, I'm a passenger in a vehicle going nowhere. Pointless thinking plagues me, and I find rest only after an extensive search leaves me still desperate. Every source of comfort I can think to hail also knows the pain of being empty, so I'm left to rediscover my home with no relief.

The taxi parks along the only stretch of sidewalk available near my oversized New York City apartment, and I get out before anything else can be said. I leave Nikki to her own explanation. The beaten concrete beneath me resembles my state of mind. Even Nikki's consolation of fair company doesn't make my defeat any less bearable. Life is changing in its degree of difficulty, and if I don't find help soon, who knows what I'll do in order to maintain control.

I look up at the streak-free glass reflecting the remaining light of day. Home stores a small collection of hope, but it will fail to last forever. When the chemicals in me permanently dissolve, I'll be a worthless man. I'm dependent upon their fading strength, and I'm ruined for it.

Even though I received a Bronze Star and Purple Heart, my medals for valor did not fill the gaping hole left in my heart when I was told I would no longer be able to actively serve my country in the military.

I walk towards my apartment and relive the devastating event that altered my life forever for the second time this week. Usually I manage to force the memory away, but I'm not so lucky the more sober I become. The wound is deep, but one day it will heal. I close my eyes and let the memory wash over me.

My only choice is the balcony window. They are coming after us, and death is certain if we do not move. Jayden and I choose our only option. The information we have is priceless, and death is the only sure way to keep their plans concealed. We both jump.

Our decision was the right one, but our cost for making it is still being paid. I continue in my steps towards home, reviewing the feeling of being forced into such drastic measures, but it does nothing to lift my spirits.

Our mission, though well-planned, was far from flawless in its execution. My brothers were ambushed at our rendezvous point just outside the Iraqi border, and intelligence unfortunately found its way into the hands of our enemy. Although fearful of the damage the United States Marine Corps can inflict, the enemy was encouraged by the element of surprise, and our recon team suffered the consequences of what can happen when you are expected.

Jayden and I were the last ones alive on our team. We would have reborn the ancient Alamo, but a small chance through a third-story hotel window gave us one final opportunity. We escaped with our lives and the testimony of what they planned next, but neither one of us expected that when we jumped it would be our final contribution to the War on Terrorism.

Mission Brasco claimed many lives but is still considered a success. I look back and the only immediate result that I can see is the knife of an emergency surgeon. I remember waking up to see Jayden and me in the same room, both with gauze swaddling our heads, arms, and legs. Snakeskin dressings were bonded neatly to Jayden's left thigh, and I was not sure why the pain silenced him, but the protruding metal from an external fixator gave me no reason to keep my pain away from others' attention.

We both sustained major injuries, losing more than eight pints of blood between the two of us. Stitches and staples lined our lacerations with precision. Tubes carrying filtered oxygen were shoved far into our nasal cavities. Both of us had multiple intravenous lines sending medications rapidly into our systems throughout all hours.

It was then I realized how extraordinary Jayden really is. The person that lay next to me, the same man at my house now, possessed character beyond training. What is admirable for some is natural to him, and his handling of our fate impresses me still. He is fearless, and even in response to such great loss he overcame and quenched the negativity surrounding him.

I recall at the time Jayden's response to suffering and my desire, if I managed to live, to mimic what I see in him. I still feel this way, but I'm no closer to the man he is than who I was that day.

The difference in our personalities aside, Jayden and I look very much alike. He stands the same six foot plus, with dark brown hair and blue eyes. The alphabet of loose scarring on his face resembles the concentration of nicks on my own, and we are often mistaken as blood brothers. We both bore the humiliation of silver tracking in our youth and reveal these priceless smiles every time we're accused.

Our build is much the same: athletic and muscular, chiseled like sculptures. Unfortunately, today neither muscle nor skill can pull me out of my slump. I trudge towards my apartment with just barely the energy it requires to meet my destination.

Jayden, although tough, is a thinker at heart. It won't be easy to hide my troubles from him as soon as he has the opportunity to look at me. A quick evaluation under his keen eye, and I'll tell on myself. None of my military training prepares me for this. If I wish to conceal my problem, I'll have to wear a mask of dishonesty again, and the thought of lying to him, above all other people, hurts.

Jayden, like me, is also honorably discharged from service due to injuries sustained while in combat. We both resent this fact, mainly because terror is still out there. We would both jump at the opportunity to slaughter this beast again, and the fact that we are bonded together with plates and screws should be insignificant.

We understand why we can no longer fight, but then again, we don't. We feel capable, but the doctors that count disagree. Their statement to the fact that certain jolted movements can have an impact far greater than we can conceive is just not good enough to tame the hearts of two truly willing Marines.

We believe we should have the choice to stay in if we can pass physical strength testing, but Uncle Sam is the final voice, and he measures our circumstance using a much different scale. Our passion for serving is still in us, but the hope of doing so is extinguished.

Having never married and with no real tie to any state besides Colorado, where I grew up, I chose New York for no other reason than that it looked interesting. I'm glad Jayden joined me, but being that he came from a small town out in the middle of nowhere, it's surprising how well-adjusted he is. I would have never guessed that this is the only other place he has lived besides home and where the Corps took him.

We rent a two-bedroom apartment in walking distance of Central Park. We are fortunate to have each other as roommates. While money is not much of an issue thanks to a few wise investments early on, New York is expensive. My largest expense, being illegal in nature, costs me more than my share of the monthly bills. It never makes sense when I balance my checkbook, but considering I haven't done so in three months, I don't think about it often enough for it to bother me.

In the little over a year since we departed from the desert sands of Iraq, Jayden has become somewhat of a crutch for me. His always content, energetic personality is a custom drug all its own, and it's shameful when I find myself dependent upon his store of strength. I'm avoiding him more and more these days out of sheer embarrassment and guilt, neither of which I know how to get around without examining myself more closely.

Right now, feelings are the plague, and I avoid them at all costs. I'm not happy, but I figure besides a gifted few, who really is?

Disappointment when I return home is the last thing I seek, but more often than not my lack of coordination speaks for me and is present without any extra effort. It isn't outlandish that he assumes I'm intoxicated. Every time he sees me, I pass the boundaries men are assigned, but I hate to know it's expected of me.

Even though I lack my usual potency, today will more than likely be no different than any other because I'm still not who I was designed to be. I give such a pitiful impression of my former self; I can't blame others for judging me.

Jayden is not the only one upset with how I'm handling life. Although I don't have an extensive family, the ones I do call kin have grown far too distant over the course of the past year.

My kid cousin Jacob is dually aggravated with me, and all I see when I look at him is my old man, Thurman Casey Shaw. I'm the Junior, but he looks more like my father than I do. A few small adjustments in his facial expression, and I feel like my father came back from the grave to scold my poor behavior.

Jacob is a 21-year-old freshman at Penn State and spends most of his collegiate weekends here with the two of us in New York City. He will more than likely also be at home and ready to evaluate my condition. The eight-year age gap between him and me does no good when I'm so blatantly irresponsible. His tall, lean physique looms over me, casting judgment simply because he can.

I'm fond of my tagalong cousin, even with his strong countenance. His juvenile boasting in hot dog consumption sparks memories of times less stressful, and his jovial spirit so often balances the serious, mature side he possesses. Between the "you-should-know-betters" I feel when I look at him and his lighthearted joking, I'm always brought back to "different is doable." He is one of the coolest guys I know. His 22nd birthday is just around the corner, and I hope he never loses this odd combination that works to his advantage.

Jacob's hair is his trademark and is as wild as his eating

habits. His dirty brown swirls of curly locks never seem groomed, but for some reason the ladies find him irresistible. He knows it, too, or so I think. Maybe it just appears that way.

He is always the first in our group to make an advance towards a table filled with beautiful single women. He enjoys leaving the clubs with an extra 20 dollars shoved in his back pocket from winning bets with Jayden and me that he can obtain the most phone numbers on a single napkin.

The fact that I'm envious of his ease in approaching those of the opposite sex does not stop me from mimicking his behavior. It seems so natural for him and so out of the ordinary for me. Even though I usually manage to scrape a few foreign-sounding names and digits on my own recycled paper, I'll never admit to my younger cousin how unbearably hard this task is for me, or that he is 10 times better at it than I am. I just won't.

I round the corner and I'm home. I open the front door and walk in quietly, hoping not to stir their interest. Nearly stumbling over Jayden's weights, I force their attention on accident. The game is on, but I grin and keep going. I'm hoping my fairly casual entry will distract them from examining me closer. My comrades look me over anyway. As they do, I open my eyes as wide as I can, trying to look keen and awake during their evaluation. My acting is poor and feels funny but is much better than the consequences of being found out.

I press my chest out a little further, as if I have pride left, and instead of joining their good time watching college football, I pass them by, headed for solitude. It hurts that I do not want to participate. Drugs steal more from me each passing day. I make it to my room uninterrupted, and it's sick that I feel relief. I'm safely behind my door where my every move will not be observed, but hiding from the ones

I care about makes no good sense.

I brush off the notion that I need help and reach inside my pocket for my phone. I resume another frenzy of rapid texting, but I'm not sure it will do any good. No one has had a surplus in days, and at this rate a drought is inevitable.

"Any kids?" I send the message guarded by code without concentrating on the many failed attempts already.

My stomach begins to growl. I'm just now realizing that in our search Nikki and I forgot to stop and eat as planned. I can't do the normal thing and fridge surf or Jayden and Jacob will know for sure that I lied to them again about my day's plans. I feel like a toddler as my mind begins filling with excuses on how I can get what I want.

I lift my eyes from my phone's screen to the full-length mirror that stands in front of me. The wife beater I'm wearing hangs loosely under my blue-and-white striped dress shirt. Even though I prefer relaxed clothing, the denim jeans I wear look more like one-size-fits-all, baggy punk pants. I can't believe what I see.

Lately, everyone has been telling me that I'm losing weight, and I have yet to see it, but now, from this angle, there is no denying the truth. They are right. I look hungry. My skin stretches tightly over my cheekbones, and the lines around my box-shaped jaw are too defined. My eyes are still dilated from a lunch of amphetamines and are black as a midnight sea. The poignant line from my favorite movie comes to mind: "If I were to be measured and weighed, I would be found wanting."

I turn away from the ghastly image, as if I can escape what is revealed in my reflection.

I make my way over to the closet, and I'm glad that I still have a small reserve hiding inside. I have been stretching my stash for days now, but I'm tired of being spent within minutes of waking up. I need a break from how many times my requests are rejected, and if it was always this way, I doubt I would have become addicted in the first place. Unfortunately, the exact moment I became dependent is not clear to me.

Once close enough, I reach down for my trusty metal box. The tattered case always serves its purpose. I have long been storing objects of great value inside it, ever since I was awarded my first blue ribbon in second grade for winning a class spelling bee. I kept that ribbon in the box for months until finally my lunch contained plastic ware too large to fit them both. I remember the choice of need versus necessity being painful even at that simpler age.

As I pull the vintage box from the bottom shelf, I steady myself against the wall. I'm growing weaker by the moment, and I decide that it's probably a good idea to open it where I feel a little more stable. I make it to my bed and remove the shoes making my feet sore. I lean back and dig through my pockets, waiting until my hand recognizes the tiny brass key that will open the container. Once I do, I shove the key far inside the narrow hole and turn it as quickly as possible.

I remove the lock from the metal clasp, and beads of perspiration begin to form on my brow. This is not a good sign. Profuse sweating is one of the first withdrawal symptoms of opium. I'm not ready for what is sure to come, and the thought of being without scares me into rushing a sure thing.

I view the contents of what I see intently. Medals, dog tags, and dope on top of a few important written documents. The pictures are few but ones that I'm attached to, and I bury them deep as I eagerly remove what I seek. My father would seriously beat me if he were alive today, and the thought of consequences later on in another life do not surface as often as they used to.

I open the bottle and consider my choice. I can take all

that remains now or save and spread, as I have been doing. Either way I'll suffer soon. I grow bitter by the second. It's stupid that I even face such a dilemma.

I ask myself what it is I plan to do, and I don't have an answer to give. Usually, drugs are the solutions to my problems; I never imagined they could run out. They seem to be everywhere, all the time, and even though I haven't been hooked for that long, I'm just as bad off as if I had been high a solid decade. I both need and want them.

I'm aware drugs are a poor choice, but I have yet to find anything else that works so quickly to numb my physical and emotional pain. While the consequences are fairly steep for getting caught with them in my possession, they have won victoriously over the penal system in my mind, as far as the pros and cons of healing a Marine's broken spirit.

I don't sit around and wonder what can happen to me or contemplate how drugs are destroying my body. I don't consider what my life would look like behind bars, nor do I believe there is any other way to function with such defeat in my life. I figure that much of my perspective should not be trusted and is naturally skewed in an unsafe direction due to the chemicals I ingest.

Perhaps if it weren't for red tape, political correctness, and lengthy medical excuses, I would be a proud, productive, clean, active Marine who otherwise would never choose such a destructive path. If I were forced to consider my behavior along with my attitude, I'm sure I would blame someone else. Hearing my own negativity and failure to accept responsibility, I wish I could escape.

Over all, opium's attachment to my life seems unbreakable, whether I want it there or not. Even though it was necessary to be prescribed such strong narcotic analgesics for a healthy recovery, it's like dynamite in my veins. I'm a man, and not only that, a Marine.

In training, I was taught to deal with pain at high thresholds while under duress, and I was more than eager to demonstrate my abilities to my superiors. On numerous occasions, I attempted to disarm and deactivate the poison flowing through me, but it was no use. Against my will, my body sent blood pressure readings to connected monitors that screamed for all to hear.

"It's pertinent," explained the doctors, after each failed attempt at freedom, that I "allow this relief."

Finally, with no way to prevail, I swallowed my pride and accepted this aspect of recovery.

Even during the physical rehabilitation phase, I was unaware of opium's cunning nature. In secret my body grafted to its promises of assistance, and in lessening my intake of narcotics, my core never again responded like it had. I was dependent and didn't even know it.

Regardless of something I could not explain, I continued to fight with all I had left. I mastered every exercise required and met every challenge the doctors posed, in pain and with little chance to succeed. I worked hard and was proud of my achievements in physical therapy, but victory was short-lived. When the gavel fell and the decision was made that I was "unable," I fell apart and never attempted reconstruction. I did nothing but serve my country well, and how it came to this predicament is still beyond me.

That day, my back grew weak under my own weight. My arms became too heavy to hold up. My heart burned with malice, and my mind made an enemy of debate. I look back and realize that that was the day I gave up and gave in. It's far easier to blend in than to be bold in the face of certain tragedies. That was the day I accepted, without conviction, my hatred toward the world and just about everything in it.

CHAPTER TWO

Take it all, or don't take it all? I look down and remove what I owe from the stash in my hand. I drop it into an empty envelope; what is left will not last. It's an odd combination of drugs in a bag, but some is better than none, and I'm happy to at least have what I do.

I pull what I need from the clear, plastic pouch and put the remaining in a bottle designed for something entirely different. I'm not excited to use the last of my preferred drug, but I won't have any energy left to search for more if I don't.

My body is aching. As fast as I can, I mix what I shouldn't, and before I think of any other fear, it's done. It won't be long before a certain relief. I close the box in my lap and lay it by my side. I relax my composure and rest against the poorly made bed beneath me. I stare at the ceiling above, and time is mine to think. I have a plan, but it's not a good one.

It includes bailing, with no explanation as to where I'm going. I plan to just get up and walk right past them, keys in hand, and head out the door. I take a deep breath, and as the seconds pass it seems like a better and better idea. The bar is only fun when I'm drunk, but what I have in me will do in order to get the information I need on what is left out there to buy.

I coerce my relaxed frame to sit up and get ready to go. I hardly feel like moving, but I've got to keep going. If I fall asleep, I'll pass up an opportunity that I can't afford to lose. I get up and return the box to its specific cove only after I reopen it and collect what is meant for another.

I pass by my bed and in doing so catch a glimpse of my keys laying in a crease made by my body's design. Next to the imprint, I see the balloon laying where I left it. I scratch an itch and pick up my trash. For the life of me, I still don't get why the tiny festive rubber is chosen to pass along a gift not worthy of celebrating. I guess in the beginning it was exciting, but it's not anymore, and the irony of that I will think about later. Now, I just have to make it past my brothers.

I take another deep breath like it's really helping me, and before I get to the door I consider that I may be going backwards, even though I move in another direction. I rationalize the familiar debate of need versus necessity. Within a second, with the help of a manipulative drug, I make a choice.

I open the door and with a gate three times my normal size, I launch myself to the front door like I'm late for the date of a lifetime. The TV is loud, and I can't tell if my name is being called or not. I can't care at the moment about anything else that might slow me down. The sooner I have information about where I can find replacements, the quicker my life can get back to tolerable.

I make it past them and stop only when standing at the door of my shiny, black, tough-guy pickup. The fear that gave me the energy to flee does not partner well with the image this machine gives. I'm not hard at work hauling tools and toys but weak at heart, aiming for escape. This, like many other things, I'll have to explain. Running off like there is an emergency and leaving them to their own thoughts of concern is just low down, and I know it. I hate being this way, but I hardly feel like I have a choice.

Hurting my family is one of the results of using drugs that was not mentioned to me as a precaution prior to use. As much as I detest admitting it, it's my experience that they go hand in hand, whether purposely intended or not. I make myself sick with guilt and swallow the remorse that surfaces.

I change the subject in my mind and think about the reason I left so abruptly to begin with. Justification for being a jerk is easier found when high. I rest in the assurance that time will ease their anxiety and head off to where I have to go.

I pull into the only vacant space the dark lot offers. I check my reflection in the shiny paint on my truck. Looking a bit wrinkled, I shake the apprehension that tries to leach onto me through my poor attire. My excuse is the rain. Tiny drops begin to fall from the sky, and as each pellet of wet weather penetrates my chemical lining, I shiver. The temperature is falling fast, and I make a run for it.

I dash down the street, rushing myself faster than normal to get inside where I can be blocked from this vicious attack. Upon entering, I brush off as many of the freezing drops as I can. Mother Nature can be rude at times. I look up after I accept that I'm wet and try and find Jimmy. The musty stench of the room clings to me, and the further I move in, the harder the rain begins to fall. At least she waited until I got inside.

Sometime in the course of the afternoon, severe weather rolled in and I had no idea. I should pay better attention. I'm now stuck here whether I like it or not. I hope I haven't caused myself more trouble for no reason.

My mind is preoccupied with the rumors of a drought. I know law enforcement has made many major drug sweeps across the nation lately, with a pointed few focusing on New York City, but I never expected them to be so accurate in their pinch.

Last week, a large crew distributing an abundance of the city's wealth of narcotics was brought down forcefully, and in the process dried up more than half of the area. They didn't just hit the corner dealers for small change; the bust will go on record as the largest sweep of major players at one time in the state's history.

With all of the king pins and drug lords removed this side of the ocean, harvesters from around the world need new importers. From my own research, I have learned that they will not be able to afford these unknowns anytime soon. They are believed to be very dangerous. Their fight for up-coming power and their instincts not trained to die for the cause slows down the decision-making process tremen-dously. No one wants to sit in jail for the rest of their life or die trying to escape.

The export of products is on hold now, the stash sitting right outside of the country until they can establish a new order. I'm not worried about the products resurfacing, just the time in which it will take for them to arrive. This process, I know, will happen with as little delay as possible since "time is money," but I can't wait forever.

While this is a war I'm not ready to be personally in-volved in, I don't mind benefiting from it. However little my involvement is as a user, I do it for reasons concerning no one but myself. I'm only here to find out the expected date of delivery and how I can be one of the first consumers testing new shipments.

I make my way deeper into the bar's belly and scan my

surroundings with the method I was trained to use in the Marines. I take mental note of what is important. I doubt this way of observing things will ever leave me. These people are not my enemies, but I don't consider them friendly, and it keeps me on edge even more than the drugs do.

I spot Jimmy, but he is not alone. He is as far away from me as he can possibly get inside the building, but I would recognize his stance from anywhere. He is lame on his right side due to a blown-out knee. I never pressed him for an explanation, but I remember Jimmy once explaining that street life is unforgiving.

I make my way over to the corner of the bar, and I feel queasy as I walk. I'm not sure what it's from, but I doubt it's the heroin making me sick. I didn't take my preferred dose, but it should have kicked the withdrawal symptoms anyway. I cringe to think maybe I so drastically decreased the amount from what I had been doing that it won't have any effect.

I meet and greet the first friend I made along my shady way. His buddies get up per his request, and I sit down to rest my nerves. I reach my hand in my pocket, and underneath the shaky table I send over the envelope made for him. I'm sure he appreciates that I return what I borrow. I sit patiently and wait to hear the update on my fate.

"What's up, man? How's it going?" Jimmy shifts uncomfortably in response to my question.

Observing no threat around him, he answers my greeting, "Not so good, man, and you?"

All I can manage without revealing my helpless dependency is: "I've been better."

I quickly follow with possibly the most common question of the day. "So what's this I hear about a drought?" Jimmy shifts again to a slightly less casual position.

"It's true. Everyone is tapped out."

Immediately I inquire to what extent this depletion exists, but in examining Jimmy's eyes they tell me the shortage is worse than I imagined.

I sit back, communicating that he doesn't need to answer out loud. Concern is written all over his face, and he knows I can see it.

"Wow, so what's the plan?" I ask this like his business is my business.

Without reserve, Jimmy gives me an answer: "I don't have one."

It's shocking to hear this, even though he probably still has some tiny sale up his sleeve. I never expect him to reveal all, but even if he is hiding a few they aren't enough to bring him comfort. I let out a sigh, not caring who understands my frustration. This is getting ridiculous, and my body is not going to keep being patient. He seconds the notion, and his agreeing with my aggravation somehow makes me feel better. I guess misery does love company, but that fact is not changing anything, and I don't have time for spiritual notations.

I look across the table at Jimmy. I'm not sure as to the degree of his dependence on drugs, but I know if he is anything like me, just the thought of reality creeping its way back into my life is reason enough to stretch my limitations in all areas.

I have noticed the similarity among addicts that no matter the drug of choice, all of them feel vulnerable. I look around. Everyone surrounding me once had boundaries they refused to cross; ones they swore they would never even get close to.

Once upon a time, I, too, had many rules, but lately, I cling to only a small few that keep me alive, and it's alarming. This sober-minded thinking frightens me.

Somewhere inside of me I begin to freak out, and my response to these emotions is to flee. I have to get out of here. The weight of the room is smothering me and forcing me to see a reality that I'm not ready for.

I jump up more quickly than I should, and the abrupt movement startles those around me, including Jimmy.

"Dude, are you alright?" Jimmy poses the question as a formality, but he already knows the answer.

We are great at reading one another. I find many addicts are quite intuitive, for necessary reasons. Knowing there is a few treasures still hiding in my closet gives me a sense of peace. I shrug an answer as genuinely respectful as I can. He nods and acknowledges the weakness I try to conceal. He motions for his buddies to return, and as they do I over-hear pieces of a bizarre tale consisting of a mystery saint out to save the lost by making them sign contracts in ex-change for their habits.

As crazy as it is, people manifest stories to make them-selves feel better, and I definitely don't have time for games. I wave hello to the new crew around me and goodbye at the same time. I don't know a single one of them, and it's prob-ably for the best.

I head to the exit, and I'm no greater for having entered. My mind wanders into a dominion of despair, and as I'm on this familiar path my head proves too far in the clouds. I do not see her until it's too late.

I smack into her delicate frame, and I can't believe I'm the one that rolls onto the floor. Laughter fills the drunken lungs around me, and my embarrassment is so great that I don't know what to do first. My attraction to her causes me to stutter as I get up and make my apologies in the most con-trolled manner I can.

"I-I'm so sorry, Indy. My bad. Are you alright?"

Indy Stokes is a person that makes you wonder why she is still hanging around this dump. Her beauty is three times the value of this place, and I've considered more than once the possibility that she might have poor self-esteem. Gossip tells me that others know as much as I do about her.

Her mom named her Indy after the Indianapolis 500, relating her labor to a never-ending race. Besides that, we know she's a cousin of no-one-knows-for-sure and hangs around because we really don't know why. Since she's always here, never formal, and continually smiling, she gets away with her habitual attendance without extensive probing. Besides, we all agree the scenery is a whole lot more appealing with her in it. We would hate to see her go on behalf of us being too nosy.

"I'm fine, Casey," she says. "It's you who fell. Are you alright?" She asks this in a very concerning tone, but the fact that she has to ask at all makes me feel like a mule.

I shouldn't be annoyed by her question, but I am. I answer way too quickly with a lie, hoping I do not come across too disturbing.

"I'm fine," I say. "Really, no sweat. I was just heading out in a hurry. I've got lots of places to go and stuff … really fast and stuff."

For the life of me I don't know why I'm so handicapped when communicating with women, and if I speak any faster she might think I work as an auctioneer. My humiliation grows by the second, and I go ahead and point to the door like a traffic officer. I'm not doing myself any favors.

"Yes, Casey, that is where you leave." She tries to ease my nervousness with light sarcasm, but it doesn't help.

Everyone is paying attention to our mishap, and the need to get out of here increases every second. I wave goodbye, and as I turn to escape it wouldn't be my reality if I didn't run into the waitress standing right behind me with a full pitcher of beer. This time my run-in leaves me soaking wet and mortified.

Fortunately, I don't hear what the whole bar thinks. The voice inside of my head is loud enough to drown them all out, and right now it's screaming for me to get out of here immediately. I obey the command and pass the waitress as she motions for paper towels.

Indy yells for me to wait up, but I ignore her attempt to help me and jet through the doorway to all the places I really don't have to go. As soon as I'm far enough away that it's unlikely I'm being followed, I look down at myself at the wreck I've become. I mutter the curses I wanted to from the very beginning, now consciously avoiding authority for fear of being accused as a drunk in public. I'm grateful that my truck is parked just around the corner; sanctuary awaits me inside.

I make it just in time to plop into the seat and notice a blob of unidentified goo stuck right next to the 6x6-inch spill on the front of my shirt. It must've happened the first time I fell; there is no way to be more embarrassed than I already am.

I crank my truck into gear and head home, worrying that I haven't been gone long enough for Jayden to fall asleep yet. Although true that it's my home, too, the alienation I feel when I'm there only comes when I'm not alone. I want Jayden around but as my silent partner, and it's safe to assume this is another selfish and unfair desire drugs reveal in my heart.

Driving home in silence does not clear my mind enough to think but allows my worries to be heard. The radio might help to silence them, in part, but my concern is too loud to drown out. I look down at the time, and I'm not sure what I would rather it be. The past is past, and what I really want is to be past all of this. I realize that in wishing to skip the present, all that can make me stronger is lost. I veer away from everything I've ever been taught, and it makes no sense to continue as I am, but I do.

I've tried once before to explain what's trapped inside of me, but when I do I have a reaction much worse than my response to females. The words don't come out at all. I just stare and hope that what ails me can be seen well enough on my face for its distinction to be recognized. The problem with this now is that the masks I wear daily do more to conceal my care than reveal my pain, and in turn I look ruthless and mean.

I don't intend to live like this forever, but right now I don't know what else there is to do. My dilemma is frustrating, and I don't fully understand it myself. Allowing drugs to rule my heart would never have defined my character a year ago. I'm everything I detest, and I'm willing to be hated just so my weaknesses remain concealed. There is barely a hint of the once-fine Marine left inside of me.

I focus on the hard time that I'm sure is coming from Jayden and realize that I'm bitter towards my country for doing nothing more than what I'm doing right now: worrying about the uncertain future. The similarities sicken me, and I try to close my mind.

I make it home safely and without the burden of police. As tired as I am, I almost wish I had all those places to go to. Putting off my reunion with Jayden for a better time is a good idea, but if I push myself more with no real place to go, I'll spend my reserve of energy poorly.

I stare at my apartment door for the second time today. On the other side will be either Jayden awake or Jayden not awake. Awake means I'll have to give an explanation I'm not ready to give; not awake means concealment for another day.

Inside, Jayden is still awake. My heart sinks, and now that I'm in forbidden territory there is no use in hiding my face. Jayden, being more patient than I can hope for, doesn't move from his seated position on our couch.

My now dirty, too-loose clothing looks like a war-torn tarp dripping with anything but honesty. A paralyzing silence fills the air, and I can't avoid his stare. This time, before he can say Checkmate, his eyes speak in a way I've never known.

From this angle, I can see perfectly that he is in pain — real, honest pain. I run over to him, searching for the source of his agony, but nowhere do I find a wound that inflicts what I know so well. I scan him over a second time, and again I see the familiar signs of something extremely wrong. Whatever the damage, it seems like torture, and when I can't find the cause, I look into his eyes in time to watch a single tear forms itself in the corner of his right eye.

I panic, thinking I'm too late and without any stopping it, it falls. I feel a sting pierce through my cloak of deception, but there is no use in trying to block out my emotion. Sorrow touches me, and I'm not ready for its intrusive attack.

"Jayden!" I yell at my brother, as though we are miles apart. "Jayden!" I yell again.

In his hand he is clutching tightly the remains of my treasured box, and it's shocking to me that I just now notice it. I don't know what to think. I can't determine what is right or what is wrong. All I feel is a storm of anger beginning to swell inside of me.

When I finally digest what he has done, I raise both hands to the ceiling and growl at the one who has wondered too far inside of my den. Jayden doesn't move a muscle, refusing to acknowledge my groaning. I continue to raise my hands, but I stop vocalizing my anger. Jayden looks as though he is dying, but it's me who is confused.

I observe him more closely and notice that his fist is clenching a small bag. As soon as I see that he hasn't destroyed it, I demand he give back what he has stolen. Without a fight, his breathing decreases, and he releases the restraint he has on my life.

My brother-in-arms, as strong as he is, will not man my life for me, nor will he try and father me down. He isn't speaking, but all is said. Neither one of us loses well. I snatch the drugs and storm off like I'm a scorned child. It takes nothing more to fully hate myself.

I slam the door behind me, and my two natures, defender and defeated, already badger one another. One is justified, and the other is not. I can hardly contain the two bickering voices in my mind, and I decide to silence them both. I look around for the 20-ounce bottle of water I left on the floor.

What kind of person am I? I bend over and pick up the noisy, half-full, too thin plastic bottle from under the corner of my bed, and I'm stuck feeling like a jerk the longer I wait. *Semper fidelis* still means something to Jayden. He doesn't know how to leave me behind. He is always faithful. The motto clings to him naturally, as though he were branded with it at youth.

How is it that Jayden is so content? Why am I not privy to the briefing on how to live excommunicated from the Corps? It's frustrating, and whether that is an accurate depiction of the truth or not, holding onto the fact that he has something I don't makes it easier to feel sorry for myself. Pity is poor, but the truth is worse.

I hear myself think and know I'm wrong. I have no more ground to stand on than he does, and in this I guess I see the point. He doesn't stand retaliating against what he cannot beat but sits and finds rest after a job well done.

I open my hand. "My name is Bitter. Life sucks and it always will."

I mock out loud the ending I feel and swallow down what remains of my stash. I'm not trying to kill myself, just purge from my memory the events of this horrible day. Hopefully when I wake up the drought will be over, and I can resume a less painful way of living.

Seconds pass and turn into minutes. Minutes pass and my problems move with them. A lighter, less taunting advocate begins speaking, and, unlike the two arguing earlier, I like the sound of her voice much better.

By the time a half hour passes, the slow descent into immoral dissipation becomes a head-first plunge into hell, and I like it. I twist every wretched thing, and it's easy to see why I enjoy drugs so much.

I hear former debates being won by half-truths, and my choice to take everything I had left proves to be a good one. I'm off the hook of every major issue I have pressing against me, and the feeling of weightlessness is priceless. I'm carefree and content to never leave this place nor ever respond to difficulty again. My complications are gone, and I drift completely into a false reality.

CHAPTER THREE

I wake up feeling hollow, in the presence of complete silence. I can't tell if it's a dream or just the truth that I'm so empty and alone. It's never still in New York. I'm aware that I'm alive, but just barely.

My stomach cramps and reminds me of its neglect. I feel around for a weight to hold me down. The only solid thing that I can grab onto is the sheets piled by my side. I find comfort realizing that I'm at home.

I try to recall why things are so unclear in my mind. I backtrack as far as my memory will take me. I try to walk through the snapshots of random events in my brain, but nothing seems to give me a solid reason as to why I feel as though I could float away. The images are scattered and unsystematic.

I continue sorting through the unnecessary clips until finally there is something in my search that tells the entire story. Seeing Jayden sitting in defeat in our living room brings back the reasons why I tried to forget. I remember now. Jayden knows everything, and I no longer have a secret to keep.

I remain motionless. The inquiry I'm sure to receive will require much consideration on my part. I know that when I emerge from my self-made prison, I can't come back and start over if I don't like how the interrogation is going. There is not enough time in the world to manifest a lie large enough to swallow the evidence before me. I'm lost and with no way to deny my addiction.

I'm interrupted by the smell of bacon in the air, which means not only that Jayden will forgive me but that he's probably home. I can't understand how Jayden can tolerate me after knowing the truth. I have no excuse. How can I explain what I barely understand myself?

No pain exists that I can describe that he doesn't also know. Jayden suffered as I did. We almost died together. We mended side by side. No way can he not imagine my struggles or my loss. My head begins to hurt.

Although the aroma of a warm breakfast surrounds me, I smell another odor that totally opposes the feelings of love and nourishment I felt just moments before. The stench, though subtle, grows stronger the more coherent I become.

I need to breathe and free myself from the clashing scents that stir the confusion around me. I yawn in offense and wait for the oxygen that I inhaled to rejuvenate me. The two conflicting smells continue to fight for dominance over one another. Unfortunately, neither one wins, and I'm not energized.

Although I find no satisfaction in my atmosphere, I'm aware of a tangible solution to my lack of energy hiding just beyond my closet door. I would have to leave my shallow pillow top grave in order to succeed, but I don't know if I can even move yet.

A thought crosses my mind that I have not considered in quite some time. *I could lie here and get the drugs out of my system and live sober again.* Before I realize what I'm thinking, panic names my tune. I have barely enough energy to breathe, much less face the new world of know-all that I have created.

I try to envision a future without a reliance on substance, but I can't see it. I think about it for a long while until I decide that I'll have to make that kind of decision later. Today, I'm weak and need a kick start.

With all reluctance quickly fading, I stretch my legs to a solid point followed by my arms. I hold for a few seconds then return to a lifeless position. I need to try that again if it's going to work out the kink I'm feeling. This time with more force, I lay into the freedoms of flexibility. While releasing all anxieties through my extremities, my hand catches on something and flings it to the floor. Hardwood makes no excuse for being loud.

Frightened by the sudden noise, I jump. As if the multiple tours in war-torn countries are not enough reason to hate crashing noises, drugs take their own toll on my central nervous system.

I open my eyes to find the source of the disaster and, as soon as I do, beams of light strike my face. Repeatedly, they beat down on the existence of the form before me. It, too, is startling. As my eyes begin to focus on the details, I find the source of the stench that opposes the warm, hearty breakfast.

Vomit leaks from the side of a garbage can that someone must have placed purposely at my side. I speak aloud to no one but myself and hear what anyone would think: *That is disgusting.* I must have thrown up after I blacked out. I want to ask who would have been so kind, but I already know the answer. Jayden is my family.

Within seconds, I'm back at the beginning, trying to seek

a legitimate explanation for the way of things. I allow sufficient time to pass, but even after infinite reasoning I know
I have nothing that will satisfy his hunger for the truth. I lift
my arm and check the time on my watch. The numbers are
insignificant because I realize that it has been over 36 hours
since I last saw myself. There is no way to disguise this kind
of issue. I'm a solid wreck, put in the very best way.

What I do know is that I would feel better if I could face
the matter numb or even downright oblivious. I pull myself
together and carefully rise from the pit of my own making.
I feel vertigo but willfully force my way through the uncer-
tainty. I stagger towards the closet with little to no strength
at all.

I manage to make it across what seems to be a manmade
maze of silk sheets, cargo pants, boots, and buckles. I can't
recall the last time I made a point to clean. I note to myself
to hire a maid.

Once I make it past the threshold, I stop to face the bad
news. All of my bottles have been discovered. I remember
Jayden finding my box, but I didn't realize that he had stolen
all of my hope. Chaos begins to break the surface of my
composure. In an instant, my solution to the world as I know
it becomes nonexistent.

Immediately, I'm back to the imaginary restraints of my
bed. Without moving a muscle, I'm confined once again to
feelings of hopelessness. *This can't be happening. I'm not
bothering anyone. Why can't Jayden just let me be?* I ask
myself these questions, and my anger energizes me.

I can feel my adrenaline soaring. It would be enough to
make it to the bacon but then what? I don't have much fight
left. I leave the room that protects me and force myself to
confront Jayden, free from the synthetic encouragement that
normally drives me.

As composed as possible, I reach the den and look around.

To my relief, no one is there. I can feel my tension free itself from the inside out. With my apprehension gone and a quick double-back to make sure, I take the seat that Jayden had recently occupied in turmoil. I realize that somewhere along the course of the last year, I became a coward. I don't know how to respond to seeing myself so accurately.

I sit with the weight of the world until my thoughts are interrupted by the source of the comforting aroma. Breakfast sits directly in front of me and changes the course of my thoughts altogether. I'm famished and here, a heaping pile of Southern-cooked sausage and bacon. Jayden knows it's my favorite.

Immediately, I shovel the logs of meat in two at a time to digest all at once. Even though it's not warm, the meat melts in my mouth, rattling all taste sensations possible. I can't recall when I last ate; I realize that I'm starving. After filling myself with every bite, I consider the trouble Jayden must have gone to in order to get this greasy pleasure. The markets around here aren't much for the South's tradition of clogged-artery delicacies, so it had to be from that special diner Jayden and I found when we were invited to the mixed martial arts free for alls.

We won $1,000 that night and slaughtered the local boys, all in the name of fun. We left a little bruised ourselves, but Jayden and I have always been excellent combat partners. Not many can succeed against us on a bad day, but if we are on top of our game, we're deadly.

Our victory stirred a fierce hunger inside the both of us that night. We wandered around the streets of New York until we found our hearts' desire. Our appetites led us to the fattiest breakfast we had eaten in the early morning in years. We loved it. The memories still feel warm.

Seconds turn to minutes, and I try to remain in the moment. The only thing that lingers is the silence of the apartment. Peace and quiet are rarely achieved in New York City, but I want to hear the ruckus of men being boys. Those were fun times. Fun now is only a memory of my past.

This thinking is beginning to hurt both mentally and physically. No way can I just sit here and wait for my future. I'll never move forward all on my own. I need chemical assistance not just for the boost of energy but for the numbing of pain, the aid in dulling my memory, and the help in regaining confidence.

Knowing where I have to go to come across my best chances, I force myself through a quick shower and half shave. I really do hope to find better luck this time. Droughts are never convenient. Still, I'm sure to find something.

Declaring this hope in my mind, I set off once again, leaving Jayden to second-guess my goings. A note would not be sufficient, so I leave no excuse for him to find. I don't want to insult him any longer. These new declarations come easier the more desperate I get.

Heading back to the spot of little help, I call Nikki, only to hear of everyone's poor condition. Sounding miserable, she hopes I'm calling with good news. Dejected, we hang up simultaneously. I try not to think the rest of the way to the bar. I'm beginning to feel nauseous, and I'm sure it's not the bacon.

Sweating and without choice, I pull over to puke. After minutes of uncontrolled humiliation in front of all who can see, I slam the door to my truck and hurry to the nearest convenience store to quench my thirst with Bismuth. My stomach exercises its right to acrobatics. In line to pay, I almost lose my composure. My insides fight against themselves—a result of my poor choices.

I declare a limit to this inner chaos, but my abdomen refuses to obey my orders. I fight hard over the next minute and a half to restrain the uncontrollable urge to waste all that's in me. The instant my feet hit the pavement outside, I hurl the remainder of my breakfast onto the concrete. It will be a horrific welcome to all who enter. I don't even care enough to warn the clerk inside. I climb back in my truck, and, moments later, I arrive again at the corner pub.

It's lunchtime at the Night Bar. If that doesn't send signals to law enforcement, I don't know what will, but we never seem to hear much from them, and no one fights to have them invited. If they are here, they're discreet and probably face the same issues we do. Addiction, I have discovered, does not discriminate by job, social class, education, or any other false hope one could believe will save them from the same fate. We are all on the same playing field and mesh well with others.

As soon as I clear the entryway, every junkie in the place who knows what I seek whistles for my attention. Unfortunately, they're filled with questions, not answers. After a few Hi's and Hello's, I settle in among Jimmy and his pals. The conversation is weak at best. I begin to feel lame. His life is no better than mine. I'm far from denial of the truth that the matter is more than just drugs.

I have unresolved issues with God. While refusing to converse with my Maker over his choice to kill my career, my rebellion brings me to the point of tired beyond my years and incapable of living my life on my own terms. I just want this misery to die, and the only way I can end it, short of falling on my own sword, is to deaden my emotions as much as I possibly can. I know it isn't the ideal way to cope, but knowledgably it's the quickest way to stop the hurt from consuming me. While contemplating other ways to obtain what I need, I recall mention of a past solution.

"Hey, ugh…" I have to gather my thoughts, while I realize what I'm asking. "Do you remember that saint dealer guy you guys were talking about a few days ago? You know, the one with the special deal to be had or something like that?"

Jimmy's sidekicks shout with laughter. Obviously, they aren't familiar with it and the very idea, comic relief. Jimmy, as buddy-buddy as he can, gives me the old "Bro, you are losing it" smile and punch to the gut every guy could do without. Ashamed or not, I brush off the urge to deck them all. *At least I'm trying,* I tell myself. I rack my brain to try and remember where I had heard the story. I begin to wonder if I made it up. Maybe I did.

The conversation continues over nothing really important. Time passes but I do not. I know I'm not crazy; I heard a story about a man who could help. That story, the more I think about it, I heard here in this bar. I'm sure of it.

"You guys sure you don't remember that guy?"

This time, the shouts become a roar that even the next booth over finds amusing. That's it. My patience can extend no more. I'm going to bust the laughing jaws of all of them, but I don't move from my seat. I know I don't have enough energy for a bar brawl, and I definitely don't have enough to fight what is sure to follow.

Through their laughter, I realize that perhaps this is why the others haven't left yet either. No one has touched the old fish sandwiches we ordered an hour ago. Our gathering looks honest enough but is far from legitimate. We're not long-lost high school buddies, old fishing friends, or a past Boy Scout troop reliving good times. We're anything but justifiable. Truth-be-known, we're all hoping on change that isn't coming, floating in and out of life on fumes.

It's decision time again. Do I leave without accomplishing my task, or do I wait around and hope for the best? I'm somewhere between deciding to throw in the towel but not quite ready to wave the white flag when something catches my eye in the rear end of the bar.

A neon flicker points the way to the restrooms. This is more than ironic to me. There is nothing peace or rest-filled about a noisy, iridescent light dancing to the beat of old 70's rock, yet it's direct.

On a whim, and desperate for change, I excuse myself to go to the bar's declared oasis. Inside, I realize the promotion outdoes itself. It's just the same stale, urinal-filled room I remember. I'll find no rest here. Needing to go, I choose a stall instead of returning to my seat dissatisfied. Sweat runs down the sides of my cheeks. My head falls into the palm of my hand, and I lean into the wall in front of me. I begin to curse everything I know. Afterwards, I expel the idea of hope. There is nothing left to look forward to.

I force myself to regain composure, wash my hands and face, and while looking back at my pathetic image I realize that I'm not alone. Standing in the corner by the exit stands a man that I apparently overlooked. My skills are shameful. Being caught off guard by his presence is nothing compared to the response I feel in hearing his greeting.

"Are you looking for something to hope in?" he says.

I'm stunned by his certainty. I dry my face on the corner of my shirt sleeve, turn, and answer indignantly.

"Excuse me?"

The tendency a man has to defend an accused weakness surfaces naturally, and the surge of energy that follows pleases me. I lift my frame once more to its full prominence, as if to intimidate him from any further accusations.

"It's not a hard question," the stranger begins. "Only hard to hear!"

Offended, I respond with interrogation. "What's it to you?"

He remains in his corner for only a second more, then proceeds to pursue me with confidence. His gaze is sure, and I'm anything but. The closer he comes, the more I realize that he does not belong to this place. Nothing about him speaks insecurity or desperation. Curiosity surpasses my need to defend myself, and I lower my stature to a more respectable height.

He moves very controlled-like the closer he comes, as though he can smell the wild I have become. Standing a good five feet away, he is no loser. Well-kept, soft-spoken, a dignitary, I would guess. He is definitely a foreigner to the likes of this place. He looks important, as though he carries the keys to a city, but clearly not this one.

"You are looking for someone I may know. Yes?" He replies directly to what I have not yet confessed to him.

Who is this character? I think to myself. Aggravation again resurfaces. His honesty in the knowledge of what I seek fuels me again to probe into his motives for approaching me with such arrogance.

"And who, sir, might I be seeking?" I answer strictly in order to hear what will follow.

As I wait for his response, I can't help but wonder why this man is here. To taunt me as the others do but to do it in a more stylish manner? Or can he truly have the answers I seek upon first arrival? Most importantly, if he possesses answers, why does he care?

I wait impatiently for his response. He stares directly into my eyes. I can't look anywhere but at the man who stands in front of me. He searches for something that cannot be shared in words. I can feel him seeking the secrets hidden behind my eyes. His probing makes me uncomfortable, and I lower my gaze to his chest. I'm afraid I'll give him the right of passage, and if that is to transpire, I'll be fully exposed in all of my weaknesses.

There is a long silence between us and, as though he makes a decision based off the calculations of what he finds, he pulls a card from his coat pocket, flips it over, and scribbles an address I have never heard of. With little hesitation, I accept the coordinates of someone he knows. I haven't become too proud to forget my condition. I'm fading fast with hardly the strength to keep up pretenses with this stranger.

I look once more into this man's eyes. Without further conversation, he departs as quickly as he appeared. I stand there alone as the noise of the bar seems to magically reappear. Within seconds the bathroom begins to fill with the after-work crowd needing to loosen their ties and untuck their shirts. I excuse myself from my freestanding position in the middle of the now-congested restroom.

On my way back, I can see that my seat is occupied by another hopeless jerk waiting for a break. "Keep it," I say aloud to myself then nod from across the room a discreet farewell to Jimmy. He acknowledges it with the tip of his hat but makes no effort to leave his own seat unattended to say goodbye. This bar, though a bit rundown in daylight, becomes a hotspot during happy hour. Its location is perfect to lure all to the quickest drunk possible.

Leaving with somewhere to go gives me the incentive to push on. Inside my truck, I reach again for the pink relief I purchased earlier. I swallow with my head tilted back in full extension and begin to hate everything anew. My anger releases adrenaline, which then feeds me the vigor that I need to move forward. I don't realize how much my emotions fuel my energy level. I can't imagine what would happen if I were able to feel everything on the drugs that I choose to use. I would be unstoppable in the midst of my fury.

I start the engine and speed out of the parking lot with my GPS already locating the address marked down by the strange man at the bar. Luckily, it's not far. I'll arrive in approximately 20 minutes, according to the electronic device which sits in my lap. The closer I come to my destination, I can see that parking is going to be a problem. New York was not designed with the traveler in mind. It's one of its frustrating defects I had not thought of when I chose a place to live stateside.

After parking a couple blocks over and fighting the consumers of the street, I finally arrive where the scribbled markings sent me. The building is absolutely normal-looking and identical to each of its neighbors. There is nothing special to cause me any excitement once viewed. Its name and street number are barely visible from where I stand below.

I buzz for permission to enter the building. After a few short seconds, I hear the electronic authorization that grants me access. I'm greeted by an overweight, elderly gentleman once retired and returned. His duty, as the doorman of the establishment, looks punishing though his smile seems friendly enough.

"Where to, sir?" His voice sounds more aged than his appearance. I pity him working at his ripe old age. One should be retired by then. He should be sitting around sipping tea and playing in his garden, while mulling over the rising cost of healthcare and the poor political climate. He should not be wasting away asking others where they are headed in life. I feel angry for him.

I quickly scoot from the entryway as a few tenants make their way past me with their hands full of carryout. It's mealtime again, and again I made no preparations to eat. The smell of Chinatown makes me queasy.

"Um," I hesitate in answering the man's demand. I'm not sure of the proper procedures about guest visitation. Needing help, I dig quickly to the inside corner pocket of my jeans where I had shoved the card with the numbers jotted on it. The man is generous and waits without irritation. Nervously, I give the chap the apartment number that appears on the back of the card.

"Three sixteen," I mumble. With a polite nod, he makes a quick note on the ledger in front of him then points to the elevator at the end of the hall. I follow the directions he gives and catch myself reading the familiar silver OTIS nameplate once inside. In seconds, I hear a dull ding declare my arrival to the third floor.

I'm closer now but closer to what, I don't know. I exit and wonder, seriously, why I'm following this stranger's suggestion. The guy never actually declared who it was I was going to see, just that it was who I sought. Thinking it over more now, I can't see how he would know who I seek. Not only that, but why did he actually believe I would follow his advice? I sincerely begin to question what I'm doing here. I think and walk at the same time.

I'm motivated by pure hopelessness. My current state is influenced by nothing rational. Listening to a stranger in the restroom of a bar in midtown about meeting another stranger that could help me with I'm not exactly sure what, was not what you might call a wise decision or even sane, really.

Still debating whether or not to abort this plan, I come to the door that claims the numbers I seek and stop. *Now what?* I ask myself a bit accusatorily. The large rectangle in front of me, like the outside of the building, is nothing spectacular. There are no distinguishing marks or notable differences from the other doors, just the golden numbers "316" and a single peephole like all the rest of the apartments on the hall.

Apprehensive, I look to my left, to my right, and back to my left again. Once I'm sure that I'm alone in the corridor, I press my ear to the door to listen. There is nothing to hear. I wonder if this is a hoax. I can't tell if the place is occupied at all. There are no welcome signs, smells of occupancy, or even an active draft to feel through the door's cracks.

I raise my hand to knock but anticipate what a person

might do if they realize an unexpected, odd man is hanging outside with his face plastered flat to their door. If it's a woman or someone elderly, they will freak out for sure. I imagine they will call the police.

Standing there, I realize I definitely did not think this plan all the way through. This scenario would not be the conversation or ideal way in which I would choose to end my day. Better judgment begins to find me, and I almost turn and walk away. I know, though, that if I do I might be walking away from the only relief left in New York City.

My rebellious side screams for me to knock. So, desperate and without further hindrance, I knock the universally approved knocking method without any additional debate in my mind. I tap three times, not too hard but not too soft. I wait for a response to my intrusion. My bravery retreats as soon as I retract my hand. I'm surprised to find that almost instantly the doorknob begins to turn.

Who will I see on the other side of the door, and what will I say? I can't believe I'm just now asking myself these questions. I panic at my lack of preparedness. It's too late to escape without knowing who is on the other side of the door. I'll have to retrieve my nerve from its hiding place but know of no way to force it to resurface.

As the door is pulled to an open position, my knees almost buckle. I don't know how I'll start a conversation about drugs with a complete stranger. I'm liable to get shot if I overstep my boundaries. With the door fully open, my first impression relieves me. In front of me stands a very ordinary guy who looks to pose no threat at all.

It's ironic to me to see that he is just as simple as the plain door in this uncomplicated and non-impressive building. I size him up and have no doubt I could take him. It's a pleasant surprise, considering I was beginning to fear a wild mobster.

He looks to be nothing special, and this is what gives me the assurance I need to step forward when he ushers me in. Once inside the apartment, I look around. It does not shock me that his taste resembles his demeanor. It's not inspiring or extraordinary in any way. It could pass as the typical picture of an average, middle-class American's home. The man stands by with his hands in his pockets and waits until I'm comfortable with my evaluation.

Deciding that I must be, he asks, "What can I do for you today, sir?"

I stand there puzzled. It must show because the man's hand emerges and gestures for me to take a seat at the breakfast table to his left. I oblige, having no real preparation for this event. Honestly, I'm almost without the energy left to stand. Exhausted by thinking too much over the last two days, I'm careful with my reply.

"I met someone who gave me your address."

He sits down in the vacant chair next to me as I speak. I expect him to pick up the next lead in our conversation, but he remains silent and waits for me to continue.

Not willing to reveal all my cards, I respond safely. "I'm looking for someone who can help me with a situation."

Past that, I'm out of any good words to say. I don't want to scare this man away if he really is the guy I'm looking for. I expect him to reply to this, for sure, but still he sits there without speaking. Either he's smart and wise or I'm dumb and insane for approaching a stranger with such foolishness. He continues to just wait and listen.

Feeling pushed to continue, all I can come up with is, "Um, I'm not sure I'm in the right place."

My cheeks flush as I sit here and once again, a wave of nausea comes over me. The timing is horrific. I begin to sweat heavily in his presence. I'll be mortified if I have to vomit in this unfamiliar place. I lean forward into my gut, trying to fight these feelings. I can tell my nervousness affects him. I definitely can't go to jail tonight. I would never survive detox.

I excuse my behavior to an unfavorable condition and go on to ask if it's a state familiar to him. The man leans back in his chair. He scratches his chin over and over with his thumb and index finger, as if this is going to help him discern the cause of my arrival. He considers his evaluations without sharing his findings.

His eyes are the tool he uses to measure the depth of my circumstance. I recognize this as the same gaze the man in the bar had when he peered, uninvited, into my soul. Even without voicing the exact reason I'm here, I can see this man knows. Uncrossing his now-folded arms, he stands, and I watch as he makes his way to a black chest used dually as a coffee table. He unclips the metal hinges and opens the lid to remove its contents. He pulls out an aluminum briefcase.

I have no clue what's happening, but the anticipation of knowing what's inside is almost too much for me to hide. I can't help but hope that this man from apartment 316 has the answers to my problems. I'm so anxious that my foot begins to tap before he even sits down with the case. I hope he doesn't notice my desperation and become repelled by it.

Once settled, I fold my hands to mimic his that now rest over the outside of the lid. I wait for what he will say next. This is turning into a weird experience that I'm extremely uncertain of. I still don't know if my actions are smart. One thing I know for sure is that I'm desperate and willing to wait and see what aid he can offer.

The next couple of minutes are awkward. We just sit here. The man is so still that I almost ask if he's okay. He looks as though he's in a trance of some sort but one that reflects a form of meditation. I have observed many new things and people over the course of the short time I have lived here, but this is different. It's unusual for anyone around these parts to be so still.

His eyes are closed and his breathing rhythmic. I almost think he's praying silently, but right as I lean forward to check on him he speaks.

"Sir, if you have found your way to me, you are hopeless and desperate. I'm willing to help you, though you must be willing to help yourself. For whoever wants to save their life must lose it."

I'm completely dumbfounded. I tilt my ears to make sure I understand him.

"What?"

The man is clear. "Once you ingest the contents of the box, you must loosen its hold on your life forever."

I listen for nothing more than to find out that what I heard was true. *Brilliant,* I exclaim in my own head. *This man has exactly what I need to end this night's misery, and all I have to do is play along with his riddles.*

"Okay." I speak with hidden sarcasm and without further hesitation.

The man knows this is not enough time to consider his proposal seriously. He begins to clarify the terms when I immediately accept again.

"I'll do it," I interject, impatiently.

With no way to force me into longer consideration, he opens the case to a mere inch and pulls forth what looks to be a contract and sets it down on the table in front of me. I glance at the parchment which is worded in a bit of old English, and without reading it, I approve its proposal with my signature. I hesitate before setting down the pen and realize I just signed a document without having read its contents in full.

I wager the justifications for something so careless in my

mind and find many excuses as to how I can back out of my obligation at a later date. It isn't that I'm accustomed to breaking promises; it's just that the required payment is impossible to render. He doesn't even know me, and none of this oath makes valid sense. The whole scenario is just too bizarre to take seriously.

I don't understand why he would ask such a thing in the first place, but I'm grateful to find relief so I make no qualms about it. In all, I'm sure that this man is not big enough to force my compliance anyway. I'm not worried past this point of thinking. I rule that bluffing in this case is legal. My admitted plan of deceit catches me off guard when it annoys me. I wasn't expecting to feel guilty about my decision.

I brush off the feelings as I land the pen dead center of our agreement with a thud. I then move the entire contract to a neutral position in the center of the table. I'm eager.

"I'm ready."

The man leans forward, taking one last look at my ruins and releases the metal case into my possession. He then excuses himself for a moment, and I'm free to make my own discoveries. Without further delay, as soon as he is no longer visible, I open the lid. The hinges extend straight into the case's upper and lower housing. Once opened, my jaw falls, my lips forming a perfect ring. The need to visit the bathroom comes over me.

Inside lies a bag of every type of pill, every shape made, and every substance formed. There are liquids, powders, dusts, and rocks inside the square box. All welcome my consumption if I choose them. There must be every type of drug ever created by man. Some that are familiar and some that are not.

Foreign languages and unknown stamps mark many of the products, but I refuse to be so bold and try them. There are plenty I do recognize. They seem to be organized in no specific order but are mapped out in single doses of each.

I cannot trust the view. I rub my eyes to make sure I'm not dreaming. No one will believe this in a million years. I'm beginning to feel a fondness for this man of wonder. It's too bad that I don't intend to follow his ordinance. He would be an alright guy if he would stop with the conundrums.

I continue to think how such an odd event led me to this place. As I search for the perfect solutions to all of my problems, I almost give credit to God but catch myself before he strikes me dead. I pull four bags from the container and one by one consume them all. Within minutes, I can already feel the nagging, torturous withdrawals begin to fade. My joints stop yelling for my attention, and my burdens in life begin to ease.

I take a deep breath as my life falls back into normalcy. I'm so relaxed that I can barely feel the chair I sit in. The effects of the drugs are potent. The higher I grow the more I think that less is better. My eyes cross and my ears ring. Even though my nausea faded early on, I disregard my stomach's new desire to forfeit what I consumed. I'm weightless and can hold my composure no more. I'm free to roam in the darkness, and without choice, into the night, I go.

CHAPTER FOUR

I wake up completely confused, lying on the flat of my back. I know nothing except that it's no longer dark. I try to pull myself together, and, with a certain amount of apprehension, I peek out of the corner of my eye. In the process of trying to focus, I stumble over the fact that I recognize absolutely nothing about my surroundings. The room is completely empty, and I can't recall my reason for being here.

Disturbed, I open my eyes wider in hopes that a larger view might shed some much-needed light. It proves to do nothing but lead to more confusion. My body is fully relaxed, but I'm restricted. I have no foreknowledge to help me land a solid assurance of why I'm present in this barren place. I can see nothing willing to help aid in the process of jogging my memory. The room refuses to identify itself.

Understanding nothing of the last hours, I'm lost. My arms and legs are barely notable. I take in the stale oxygen

of the room and demand my hands find my face. I figure if
I rub it hard enough, I can wash away the unsettling reality
of what I saw. My attempts prove unsuccessful. I settle for
removing the sleep from my eyes, along with a quick run-
through of my hair.

Waking up in strange places isn't the oddest thing that has
ever happened to me, but waking up in a completely vacant
room that I'm sure I've never seen is near the top on the
weird scale. There is literally nothing in the room but the
mattress I lie on.

Concern proves its need all around me. Even the bed supporting me has no sheets for protection or comforter to comfort. I continue to look around but find nothing worthy of
taking note. I can't recall a thing because I'm sure I have
never been here before.

Concerned with my vulnerability, I sit up but not without
a lag of some sort. I forfeit an audible, "Oh," without any
purpose other than to demand my stability. Maintaining my
balance is not as easy as I assumed. While attempting to
reposition, I give more effort than needed and accidentally
overextend myself to the point of finding my face near my
feet. I catch myself in time to avoid the fall, but I'm not
pleased with what comes next.

As soon as I'm vertical, a headache follows that I'm sure
came from Hades itself. I'm hungover and not the good
kind. It will require more drugs to remove this type of throb-
bing.

Again I try my best to recall the circumstance which
landed me here in such a mess. While scratching my head
to force the last cognizant memory, I groan in response to
where this push leads me. Usually a smell or sound triggers
such thinking, but this time I can blame nothing. I carry myself through my distant past, and I'm shaken to see it so
vividly.

I can barely identify the man running towards me. The waves from the chopper's heat and the sand that spin all around camouflage his entire profile until he's only inches away. I can feel Jayden's will for me to fall back within seconds of his arrival. I have only just come to help the supply drop unload when we are forced to respond to an ambush of RPGs and small firearms. The potent rounds from a distant Ak47 first signal our problem, and within seconds I notice the man beside me fall to his knees.

The remainder of us, though stunned, immediately seek cover from the deadly ricochets. The large chunk of metal in front of us does not seem great enough to conceal us all. We hold not only our position, but the hope that each bullet that flies past will not penetrate our shield of protection. We are sure of nothing and unprepared for the sudden assault. Explosions and rapid fire make it nearly impossible for us to communicate verbally, but when I see Jayden it becomes irrelevant. I know we're in trouble.

As soon as he arrives, he signals for the others to seek cover nearby and points the way to safety. He knows I'll refuse to leave the man in front of me alone, and with only a glance he agrees to help me carry him to security. It looks as though he has been hit twice, once in each leg, which makes it impossible for him to escape with the others for regrouping.

I'll never forget the relief I see in the man's eyes when he realizes that he will also gain shelter from those who wish to harm us. Jayden and I each grab an arm and lift him off the ground. His cry of pain does not deter us from slowing the pace of his rescue. We have no time to transfer him in ease, for fear of being hit ourselves.

With all of our might we run, carrying the young Marine as fast as we can, and, in the midst of his appreciation, I see something else that will also never leave me. Only feet from

our destination, the man's whimpers cease. Instead of looking to find what I fear, I look to my brother for confirmation.

I do not need to see the new wound to know that he has
been shot again. While the life fades from the injured man,
I watch as my brother sees him off from this world to the
next. Jayden does not look away for even a moment. He
trusts me to lead the three of us to the building that will be
the last place the man ever hopes to go.

Once inside the structure that is now being used as our
new fighting position, the others immediately come to help.
Knowing his fate, we surrender his body over without any
words. Death is a discovery that even a heads up does not
prepare you for.

I continue to watch Jayden's reaction. His eyes weight the
two of us down, and, in seeking where he went in his own
soul, I tremble at being along for the ride. Jayden's face is
painted with torture, and his body speaks a helplessness that
I cannot fathom.

I watch as my strong and courageous brother becomes a
mere tiny child. In hitting his knees in the middle of the
chaos all around, his cries are aimed at God above.

I never understood how he could believe in the relevance
of God in a moment like this. We never speak of what we
failed to accomplish that day, but the inability to save that
man is a burden we both carry from that day forward. Good
men dying on foreign soil is never a glorious thing. Over
time, I have seen humanity at its foulest levels in war, and
few leave from this point here unaffected.

Memories of Iraqi quests have frequently appeared in my
mind's eye over the course of the last year, but not usually
while I'm awake. My heart breaks every time I revisit that
particular failure. In Iraq, times were unfair and our circumstances heinous, but they were for a cause that was worth
fighting for.

This battle I fight in the middle of this abandoned room is for a half-life existence. I fight to participate in a world already scavenged. There is nothing lasting about the highs I seek so desperately. They do not allow a future of hope.

I sit on the edge of the bed and look around at the new war zone I occupy. I rub my hands over my battle scars. Each textured ripple serves as a constant reminder of the former life I no longer know. In recognizing these painful memories, I understand that I've ventured far into my past and that I cannot stay there. I'm no longer worthy of the medals we earned, and envisioning myself as a hero only confirms the distortion of my true reality. My life is twisted, and I'm no conqueror.

Disgusted with myself, I try one last time to recognize the empty scene around me. As I do, my phone begins to vibrate, signaling an incoming text message. I'm shocked to feel that it's still attached to my clip and is not dead. Curious to read the message, I unclip the phone from its protective case on my hip and begin to examine the blurry communication.

"Droughts up. Thirsty?" was all it said.

At once I remember the last week's events. The Night Bar by night, the Night Bar by day, Nikki, Jayden, Jacob, Indy … and I stop myself there. After recalling all that transpired, I'm ashamed all over again. I humiliated myself, and it wasn't just in front of Indy.

My actions were repulsive, and I don't know how I'm going to face the people I care about in my life. Refusing to speak to some of them will be okay for a few, but the others will require communication and reasoning on my behalf.

I know I don't possess the energy needed to debate, and, honestly, I have nothing worthy of defending. The effort I do have is pledged to finding drugs to cope. Without the drugs to cope, I have no power in me at all to fight. This depressing cycle reveals itself clearly, and I cannot deny its prevalence in my life.

Without chemicals, my body has no strength to labor towards any goal, no matter how simple or great. My thoughts are all over the map, but dead center is an issue that, if not corrected, will distort every path I choose. I have no idea how to escape this misery. I can't come up with an effective solution to solve my dilemma. I know that just acknowledging my problems and addictions are not enough to fix them.

Eager to get on the move towards a security blanket of chemicals, I stand a little more cautiously, then I choose to sit up. I wait patiently for all my faculties to catch up with me. As soon as I'm sure that I can trust my own abilities, I turn and am glad to shed the memory of this abandoned room forever. While entering into a hallway, I notice the bathroom to my right. What I see in passing stops me from moving forward.

I catch a glimpse of a man I don't recognize. A bit startled, I back up to realize the image I see is me. Disturbed, I draw my face closer to the oval mirror that hangs above the porcelain sink and dare not ask it a question. Looking at my reflection reminds me of the dead man we carried.

I'm shocked to see my eyes looking like pitted olives. The hollow center accurately describes the hole that lies within. I gawk at how visible this missing piece is. I turn the faucet on immediately and try to wash the evidence from my appearance, but nothing can erase the obvious. This must be what the man at the bar could see.

At this instant, I realize I remember more. The man in the bar led me to an apartment. That apartment must be the one I'm in, or is it? As I ask myself this new line of questioning, I poke my head around the bathroom's entryway to peer at what is left to see. In front of me stands nothing; no one lives here. There are no pictures on the walls, no clothing or linen lying around, no hygiene products or even garbage to sift through.

The apartment I remember from last night was furnished. Granted it was not extensively decorated, but it was definitely settled in. There is nothing confirming this place to be the residence that I was in last night.

The next question comes naturally and is logical. *What happened to me after I arrived?* I decide to search around for answers. I walk the entire length of the living room into the tiny model kitchen at its end. I open every cabinet door and am disappointed to find nothing of assistance. I move on to check the pantry, which also proves to be no help.

Frustrated, I march nearly to the end of the tiny circle I made and haphazardly find my answer without much extra effort at all. On the other side of the tiny bar, on the only other piece of furniture in the entire home, is my own name scribbled atop a piece of paper. It lay neatly on the outside of an old leather-bound book.

With a sudden flood of memories, I realize this is indeed the apartment I was in last night, minus all the furnishings. I remember sitting at this very table with all the worry in the world. It's not the crisp memory I would hope for, but it's enough to validate that I never left this place. I'm puzzled. I don't know how to compute this new information. How does one remove everything they own in a single night, by themselves, without waking a sleeping stranger?

I want to solve this mystery in my mind, but I have not forgotten an even weightier concern that actually has a remedy. The drought that was frustrating my life is over, and as soon as I make my purchases, things can get back to normal. I look around one more time to take in what is left to discover. All that remains are three metal chairs, the table, and my new book.

Satisfied that I can absorb nothing more, I tap the outside

of my pockets to assure myself that I still have my keys. To my relief, they're there along with my wallet, which confirms the man from last night was not a thief.

In disbelief, I go ahead and open my wallet to make sure. I'm pleased to find my alarm an overreaction. All cards are present and accounted for. I glance at the time on my wrist watch and note that the banks will open shortly. I plan to go big, and my justification is that I survived a nightmare of a week and have even more to overcome as soon as I return home.

As I leave, I have a strange feeling that I can't shake. It resembles that of guilt, but my conscience is so unclear lately it's hard to determine whether it's sending me away or telling me to stay. I dust the tiny inclination from the lining of my mind and chalk it up to a sketchy reaction to whatever it was I took last night. I collect my thoughts and give no extra consideration to this internal council, or its uncertain advice. With my new book in hand, and somewhere to be, I leave in a hurry.

I step back once more into the hall with the golden numbers. I note from where I'm leaving, turn, and watch as the series dwindle until arriving at the elevators near the end. Once on board, I push the button that's required and pull my phone into view. I figure that the dealer closest to the bank will be best for ending my search quickly.

I'm in such a hurry that I send the message of my up and coming business before I even hit the ground floor. I'm in a rush, and things seem like they can't happen fast enough. Stepping off, I can't remember which way to turn, but as soon as I exit and look to my right, I see the face I once pitied. The doorman from last night sits hunched forward in a chair behind the information desk, fast asleep. He is of such advanced age I half want to check his pulse as I walk by him but think it a tiny bit rude and pass on the notion.

Outside, joy is not my first reaction. I step into real daylight and real problems. The streets are already busy, and I have no idea where I parked. I rack my brain for clues on which way to go, but nothing comes to mind. I'm not even sure about what street I'm on. These are the unfortunate side effects of my lifestyle, and it reminds me of how stupid I am in my decision to do drugs.

My aggravation at myself is so bad that I get on my own nerves as I wander from corner to corner. In my anxiety, I receive another chime on the side of my hip that distracts me. It's another incoming text message, but this time not one so inviting.

I open the message to read that a single "X" has been sent to my phone. This is in response to the text I had sent only moments earlier on the elevator. I sigh, knowing that it's a denied request. I reason that this is no big deal and not a problem with the many of willing dealers across New York City, but it shows that I'm lying to myself in how much it affects me.

Between being lost and not having a plan, my aggravation grows so big that it resembles a swollen fury that can easily be identified as rage. My anger continues to breed hostility the longer I stroll along the streets trying to find the elusive parking deck where I left my vehicle.

My irritation grows until my grip is so tight around my phone that I suddenly remember that I used the GPS to track my way to the apartment to begin with. So often these days, I prove to be not so bright. I retrieve the map history and the little red icon that leads the way fast becomes my new best friend. I follow its direction and magically, with only a few turns back in the same direction I came, the concrete parking deck appears out of nowhere, or so I'll believe for dispute's sake.

Once I'm under the overhang, my truck is easy to find. I

hold my keys to the base of my chin and wait for the alarm to sound the way to its exact spot within the deck. As soon as it's in view, I disarm the security system, hop inside, and toss my book to be a passenger in the seat next to me.

A bit of excitement fills my spirit. My newfound luck is already proving to spread a much-needed hustle. It's now time to visit the bank and further the delight of my day. I'm ready to restore my stash and replenish the depleted levels in my system. While buckling in, I'm relieved that unlike the last time I was in my vehicle, I'm not deathly ill. I turn over the engine and eagerly pull off in the direction that will give me the funds I seek.

After standing in a fairly short line at the bank, I'm back outside and ready to resume my quest within only a few short minutes of my arrival. With a couple thousand dollars in hand, I plan to visit Bart. His quality is always good along with his quantity, and I feel it's a win-win situation. Since he does not allow you to call him, I'll have to go over and make my request in person. Even though it's a bit aggravating, I cannot justify it being a problem since I'm somewhat desperate.

As I drive towards his direction, I think about how all dealers have their own personal ways of feeling safe. I remember early on how I learned this lesson the hard way. After a few fights within the first week, I finally understood that if I was going to choose to use drugs on a regular basis in this city, I must learn their ways or forfeit being served.

Bart's preference isn't the most convenient, but considering he lives just a few blocks over and it's moderately close to my apartment anyway, I choose not to see this negatively. He is usually in good supply and trips to his place are rarely ever wasted.

As the thought of home resurfaces in my mind, I fear going back to face Jayden. I'm willing to, but only after I have chemical support. I can't handle the discussion that is sure to take place while of a sober mind. Jayden's face is always filled with a concerned expression, and looking into his pierced eyes and knowing that in my hands is the cause of his affliction, will rip me apart. I can't take seeing him this way again.

Backtracking causes more grief than normal. I almost want to weep, but I couldn't find the tears even if I tried. It has been so long since I have suffered any real emotion in its fullness. I stuff my regret into the corner of my mind and decide to bury my feelings in song. I reach for the earpiece that attaches to my phone and shove it far inside my ear. Seeking a new direction in thinking, I play the lyrical stories of other men. With their melody, I block out what is left of my sensitivity and consume all the artificial hope their imaginary world offers.

While listening to the sounds of an electric guitar, I pull up to the halfway point between home and Bart's. I reason it wise to park somewhere nearby. I feel this is the only safe way to avoid a confrontation that I'm not quite ready for. I consider the walk time and find my decision easily executed in a nearby lot.

As soon as my truck finds permanent rest, I jump out, ready for the stroll it requires to arrive at my destination. As I do, a nasty gust of cold winter wind smacks me directly across my face and nearly pushes me back into the cab.

I can tell these winds are too brutal to walk in alone. I dig quickly through the contents of my backseat until I find a jacket willing to lend itself to the occasion. This, along with a swig from a travelers bottle of Listerine, and I'm ready to proceed with my plan.

Though my mind is not as adrift as it was moments ago, the music that continues to play in my ear helps me maintain a reasonable pace. I'm fast regretting my decision to slack on my usual 5K run in central park with Jayden. It's blister-ingly cold, and I'm so out of shape that running through it seems twice the effort.

Half frozen and in more time than anticipated, I finally arrive at Bart's place. Respectfully, I knock on the door as soon I walk up, knowing that he doesn't like people hanging around. Even though his building is not in fear of being rec-ognized for crime, he is still conscientious of his appearance to his neighbors. His reputation is actually fairly respectable, and, unlike many, he plans to keep it this way.

The second I knock, the door opens. Bart has cameras out-side of his building and is already aware of my arrival. I'm sure he has been bombarded since news is out that business is flowing smoothly again, but I have no worries that he will take care of me. Bart is a business man and loves money, so he is always well-stocked for busy days.

As soon as I step inside, Bart comes toward me, offering a fist bump.

"What's up, man?" I say as I pull back from his notorious greeting.

Bart's response is typical and nothing less than what I ex-pect from him.

"Not much," he says. "I'm glad to be back in operation, without a doubt."

I respond by keeping my conversation light and smooth, trying not to reveal my overly eager appetite. "I bet. Every-one was in a bad way. I expect you're glad to see me, though."

I grin through our small talk as I pull out the two grand from my pocket, hoping that it will speak for itself. I con-tinue by exclaiming, "I'll wage even higher that the delight is more mine."

While mentally trying to calculate what all I plan to get, the next thing he speaks causes my heart to skip a beat.

"Sorry, man, you're on the list."

My eyes shoot from the cash to his face in a split second. "What list?"

Even though I semi-understand him the first time, he makes mention of a barricade. I need him to put words to what I fear. He steps back and squares his position to mine. Bart is a friendly enough guy, but personality aside he doesn't kid around about his dealings.

"Look, when I went to my guys, they called you by name. When they say a name, you are off limits ... period. We don't sit around and discuss it. I'm not sure why you no longer have privileges, but it is what it is and you don't. There is no negotiating this." He pauses, then says, "I'm sorry, man. I can't help you. I'm sure if you think about it, though, you may know more than you realize."

At this point, I can do nothing but stand here in front of Bart and consider. What do you say to something like that? I don't meddle around in this city. I have no enemies or outstanding debts. I don't deal to support my habit or loiter on possessed street corners. I'm in shock at what came out of this man's mouth and that it's directed at me.

I don't even know what to say in response besides, "Seriously?"

Bart's nod is all I need to see to know that he is, indeed, serious and plans on honoring his supplier's demand. The heat from my face forces me to consider an early retreat that I was not expecting to have to make. I'm so mad and know that if I don't leave now I might later regret my choice of action in response to this news. I have never been mistreated like this before, and now that I'm less than equal to the common user, I'm in the kind of trouble I can't buy my way out of.

This new philosophy that money no longer talks is blowing my mind. Money always speaks in this city, and I have plenty. I can't understand why I'm being refused.

I leave and, in doing so, I feel no true ill will directly towards Bart. It isn't his fault but rather his supplier's demands. I realize the business aspect of a poor choice in screwing over a hand that feeds you. I know it's unwise to oppose and tempt those in power, and I also know that he would have taken care of me if he could.

I wait until I leave his building before I make my next attempt. Even though the news I just received is quite plain, I'm not going to keel over and quit. This next one I can call. I know if he answers he is straight and ready to deal, and if he doesn't he is busy. I also know that if my call goes straight to voicemail, he doesn't have what I want anyway. Fear will only come from being constantly ignored. If my call is avoided more than twice, he does not plan to do business with me.

Knowing this dealer's rules gave me a little apprehension but not an overwhelming amount. This character is needier than Bart. He requires the money he earns in order to make rent every month, and I'll do nothing but help him earn his keep.

Once out of Bart's view, I again pull my phone from my hip. I immediately scroll through my contacts until I find the number that will become my third attempt of the morning. Heading back in the direction of my truck, I push the send button as I walk. I hold my breath and wait for the outcome of what the dialed number will bring. The phone begins to ring, and I feel a fraction of relief.

Over the course of the last few weeks, more than a few numbers have been changed and even worse, disconnected. But as the seconds pass, this tiny bit of hope begins to dissipate. No one answers. Victor's voicemail picks up. I listen as the typical numeric recording of his telephone number plays in monotone in my ear and hang up before it prompts me to record a message.

I can't believe what I'm hearing. There is no way he can afford to avoid me. In my bitter amazement, I try to encourage myself by assuming that he has only just stepped away from his phone for a brief second and that when I call back he will apologize for my inconvenience.

I'm not sure how long I can keep this positive thinking up but figure a good five minutes will be ample time for him to complete the task he is doing and answer my call. I decide to wait out of a forced courtesy before calling him back and trying again.

The next 300 seconds seem like an eternity, and I pass this time with a forward march in the direction of my truck. I pull the hood of my jacket over my ears, and I'm glad to know I'm only another 60 seconds away from warmth.

I just can't make myself understand why "they" have chosen to blacklist me. I force myself into a speedy pace as a breeze continues to pick up all around me. I'm suffering with brutal anticipation, and the only way to get relief is to try Victor again.

I stop where I stand and redial his number. My hope grows as the phone rings. This means that without a doubt he has the drugs I seek. But as I wait, the phone rings and no one answers. This time the message is set to a personalized greeting that pulls from me the worst feelings of disgust.

"Yo, this is Victor. Leave a message at the tone."

It's followed by a harassing, high-pitched beep that makes me cringe. I'm so angry I nearly crush the device in my hand again. I'm glad I make it back to my truck in time before making a scene. As soon as I'm inside, I throw what offers me no satisfaction to my side, place my hands on the center of the steering wheel, and yell with every bit of wind in me.

I don't know who I'm screaming at, but whoever it is, I
shout loud enough so that they can hear me wherever they
are. I'm furious. My face burns and the vessels in my arms
begin to show their agreement with my need to explode. I
continue to curse them for everything they're worth, but I
still have no clue who I hate or why they chose to target me.

I don't accept what I'm hearing. Another refusal and a refusal that says don't call back, at that. It's a third confirmed
denial, and it's just barely noon. I can't figure out what in
the world is going on. While I'm okay right this second, it
will not last forever, and I know it. I need to have a steady
supply of narcotics in order to avoid the tortures of withdrawal, and I need much more than just a typical dose when
I make it home to face Jayden.

Wicked thoughts come to mind, and I try my best to expel
them. I'm freezing and the more I think about it, hungry and
thirsty, too. I make a decision to visit the small café at the
end of the street. It's a short distance and will draw me out
of the futile pattern of thinking I'm trapped in, at least for a
brief moment. I need a fresh perspective and a chance to re-
group. I take a deep breath and almost jerk the handle off
of the door as I leave the driver's seat. The sting in my hand
reprimands my haste.

I trudge uphill and feel exhausted upon entering the café.
My exertion distracts me for only a second. I pause to take
in the sweet smell of cappuccinos and breakfast cakes. The
Danishes smell delicious, and in realizing that I have not
eaten in quite some time, I decide to order their House Special, no matter what it is.

I look around and choose a booth near the far corner to
sit. It's the most secluded and a place that I can sulk without
any unwanted attention. Shortly after placing my order, I
decide to call Nikki to see what she knows about what's
going on. As much as I want to deny there's anything wrong,

it's not typical to be refused in this way. My reputation is good, and this is inconsistent with anything I have seen over the course of my time using. I have no remedy and barely understand the issue before me.

When dialing Nikki, it's pleasing to hear her answer the phone after only one short ring.

"Watcha doing, Case?" she answers. She's wasted.

She only calls me "Case" when she's too relaxed to sound my name all the way out.

"What's up, Nikki?" I respond without the least bit of enthusiasm.

She answers me honestly enough. "Oh you know, a little bit of this and a little bit of that. How about you?"

The question bites. I can barely pull the words out of my mouth and reply to what she asks. "You know me."

She laughs, having no clue that I'm majority sober. The remnant of what lingers in my system is quickly fading, and just hearing how carefree she is brings about an envy in me that I know is unjust. It's not her fault I'm without.

Acknowledging that I'm feeling this way, it's best to get off the phone with her. She will not be much help anyway. Her reputation is as bad as what mine apparently has become. She seems to run tabs with everyone we know, always short-changing them when payment is due. They will know something is strange for sure the minute she walks in with a couple thousand dollars and will probably confiscate it for an outstanding debt. One thing speaking with her does do is tell me that, indeed, the drug supply is back in full effect on the streets of New York.

Processing all of this new information, I let her go with the ease of a very shallow lie. I reason against it, knowing that this will help me avoid saying something I'll later regret and probably something that she truly doesn't deserve.

I hang up and my thoughts don't stop. I'm now officially

livid. She is usually the last one of priority, and if she has scored, I'm in trouble. This thing that is going on with me, whatever it may be, is larger than what I first imagined. This news is seriously troubling.

I sit facing the empty booth in front of me, feeling abandoned. Fear takes the empty seat by my side and provokes in me the toxic "What ifs?" What if I never find a fix? What if last night is truly the last time I'll be high? What if I have to face Jayden alone?

I ask myself these things knowing only time will tell my future. Having never been known as patient, I'm unwilling to accept this decision is left in the hands of fate. I scroll through my contacts I have yet to try. There are still a few more options available, and I hold on to this small piece of encouragement.

In the middle of my clinging, a very pleasant waitress interjects an excuse for her intrusion into my personal space. Though different from the first, she leans over and serves my choice order with a sweet smile of courtesy. It's evident that I feel annoyed, but she is gracious and allows me all the time I need before returning to accept a form of payment. When she does, I hand her my debit card, and upon her agreeing to return shortly, I examine the woman more closely.

She looks to be my age but in poor physical health. She walks with a limp, and her left leg turns slightly in towards her right knee. Viewing her from a distance, I wonder how she manages this permanent defect, and even more, how she does it with such joy. Truthfully, I wonder how she walks around with such peace about it. My injuries infuriate me. They talk to me when I lie awake at night. They promised to fade and over time they did, but as they merged into my skin, they secretly grew deeper, ensnaring my soul.

Without warning, my spirit sinks to its lowest possible

depth. I try to force myself away from the enticement of self-pity, but it seems so easy to feel sorry for myself. I compel my inner being to remember my choices. I speak my accountability out loud, but this great tool of positive self-talk neither cures me nor makes me feel any better. I question the accuracy of popular literature. It's not working, and the world is a liar.

I realize the majority of my current damage is self-inflicted, but I use even the smallest opportunity to shift blame. I pause. I don't have to consider more to understand that even if I pass the cause of my problems off on to something else, it will not resolve a thing. Who cares who's responsible for it? It's done and pleading verbally to myself can do nothing more than tickle my ears with false truths.

Hearing my cynicism, I realize I've become a bitter pessimist. I never intended to be the so-and-so-someone-knows who made it out, only to kill themselves once home. But my story is easily writing itself down this road of lonesome misery, if I declare it so or not.

Wishing I could make the words I say magically fix my errors, the waitress returns with my receipt, extra napkins, and the kind of sweet smile that reminds one of their grandmother. I thank her twice for the hospitality. I'm glad for her interruption. It seems nothing can pull me away from my futile thinking. It isn't helping me to focus on my problems. I need answers.

I brainstorm with the remaining cells I have still functional. In doing so, I can't get over the charisma the woman carries with her. It isn't very often you see this kind of genuine charm. I appreciate her soothing tone for many reasons. I'm quickly growing intolerant of what's happening to me, and I'm just barely able to maintain composure. Her gentle spirit settles me so much that I wish I can capture some of her magic as my own.

I sign the white copy of my receipt and forfeit a smile. Before standing to leave, I take only a few seconds to stretch, zip, and fasten all that is left undone. Just as I do, I hear a loud crash from the café's coffee bar only a few feet behind me. I look over my shoulder to see the source of such commotion, and my new favorite waitress is lying in the middle of a mound of fresh coffee cakes and pastries.

Immediately I make my way over to rescue her from the offensively hard floor. In doing so, she thanks me and asks what she can do to repay me before she is even solid and back on two feet. Who considers another before they are even balanced? The impression she gives makes me marvel.

As I help to stabilize her, she calls herself silly and easily distracted from where she is going, but I see no humor in her fault or an absence of focus. She seems strong and tough. Her demeanor makes this no secret. I want to question to what she credits her ability.

Casually brushing herself off, she asks for my name. I hesitate only out of surprise then oblige with a weak, "Casey. Casey Shaw, ma'am."

"Well, Casey, Casey Shaw, I'm forever grateful. Today you are my hero."

I blush in response. It has been awhile since I've felt worthy of thanks for anything, and my lack of confidence around people of the opposite sex surfaces in reaction to her compliment.

"Um, anytime, ma'am," I say. "Sorry I couldn't have forewarned you of the tear in the rug."

She looks over to see that the rug in front of the counter does indeed have a tear along the edge and flashes a surprising grin.

"Well, you're right," she says. "I'm only half as clumsy as I believe."

Again she exposes her teeth, both top and bottom. She

shocks me by how she handles the embarrassment. How does she manage to grin and bear the pain and humility and not get pissed off at the world? I have to know. So when I see she is clearly okay, I feel emboldened and ask for her secret.

"Excuse me, ma'am," I say. "I must know. How do you do it?"

"Sorry?" she says. "I don't follow."

I ask again, though this time I explain what I mean. "How do you not let your loss control your thoughts?"

She smiles at my curiosity and sweetly begins to tell me her story, when I hear a shout from somewhere in the direction of the kitchen.

"Sarah! Sarah!" yells an impatient man who she seems to recognize.

I look and see the culprit interrupting my very important conversation and beg her to disclose her secret before she leaves.

"I'm sorry, I do have to go, but the answer is I keep a motto. It's Jeremiah 12:5. Bye now."

That's all she says before she waves farewell. I watch as she stumbles in the first few steps leading away from me, then instantly disappears behind the room's papered wall.

"Jeremiah 12:5, Jeremiah 12:5, Jeremiah 12:5" I repeat her reference out loud to make sure I hear and record it correctly in my mind. If I'm not mistaken, this address can be found in the Bible. It figures she would give glory to someone other than herself.

I think it over once more and realize that her faith suits her nicely, but I was hoping she would have offered a more ideal solution. If Sarah only knew that God is clearly against me, she wouldn't have suggested such nonsense.

CHAPTER FIVE

B ack to square one, I rest in my cab for a moment. I don't really have a plan, so I sit combing through the details of the day. I'm not sure what I hope to find in reliving this strangeness, but as I skip around from event to event, I realize that I have yet to open the leather gift with my name taped on it. I look around for it.

On the passenger side floorboard, I can see only the edge of the book. I bend over as far as I can to reclaim what is mine. I feel around until the book is in hand. I pull it up and force myself into a more comfortable position. I recline my seat as far as its design will allow and adjust the temperature in my truck. This is going to be interesting.

Even though I'm holding an actual book in my hand, this all seems a bit surreal. The fact that it was left for me in such an odd way is a story all by itself. I only wish that I could fast forward to see the end of how my story plays out.

I realize this notion is impossible and see the absurdity in wishing for something that I can't obtain. I know that it's not that uncommon to want to see the future, but it's ridiculous to live waiting for a vision that will never come.

I examine the cover more closely, and even though the letters are extremely worn and the cover is in poor condition, I can make out the words "Holy Bible." I nearly drop the book in my lap.

"Cute," I say out loud. "Real cute."

Someone is playing a very grandiose prank and its comedy revolves around me. I can't imagine who in the world would play a joke so elaborate; not only that, but how are they managing to get strangers to participate? Last night was bizarre, to say the least, but this is too much. There is no way anyone could have known that I would ask Sarah such a question, or that she would declare Scripture as her motto.

I decide to amuse myself and read the passage the young woman mentioned, just for kicks.

"If my memory serves me correctly, sweet Sarah, you said Jeremiah 12:5."

I continue to speak aloud, sarcastically, as if an audience is following along hoping to confirm their own suspicions. I page through in no purposeful direction. I have no idea where to find Jeremiah. I retreat to the ease of the Table of Contents. Secured with a page number, I make my way chronologically until I find the book I seek. My eyes dance from verse to verse until Sarah's motto is in front of me:

If you have raced with men on foot and they have worn you out, how will you compete with the horses? And if you stumble in safe country, how will you manage in the thickets by the Jordan?

I laugh out loud. That makes absolutely no sense at all. The heading reads: "The Lord's Answer to Jeremiah." The woman can barely walk, much less run, yet she stumbled in a safe place. She will clearly never make it through any thicket I have ever seen, and who challenges a beast to a sprint?

Amusement strikes me where I sit, and I feel an unlikely humor come into play. I stretch a much-needed chuckle to its limits and throw the book back to its place on the floorboard. Someone sure went to a whole lot of trouble to make me laugh, and it dawns on me who it could be: Jimmy.

I can't believe he is going to these lengths to one-up me. His personality is growing, and I realize he is capable of much more than I give him credit for. It's such a dishonest treachery that I would question our friendship, but no one in the drug world lives under a pure moral umbrella, and I have learned not to expect much more than a C minus in conduct from anyone.

The majority live in a corrupt state of mind most of the time. They embrace the depravity of man as a normal and acceptable occurrence that excuses them from having to display any and all manners. Their sense of loyalty is somewhat nonexistent, and I don't know why I feel surprised.

As much as I hate to admit it, he really does have me thinking I'm on a blacklist, and, even worse that, there is a man running around giving away dope to poor schmucks like me on a regular basis. I'm sure he is to blame for my confusion. He is the only one who can successfully coerce me into following a stranger's direction for illegal treasure.

What a jerk. I grin in a perverse sort of way. I can just barely see the humor behind it all, and I'm definitely going to enjoy the art of retaliation. I relax for the first time since all of this commotion began. Jimmy is to blame, and I can take care of him with only one of his famous gut punches required.

I'm suddenly filled with spontaneous motivation. I can't wait to get to the Night Bar and declare my knowledge of his sophisticated scheming. I start planning my entrance.

It's a tossup between bluntly declaring myself as no one's fool, or participating in a fresh farce myself.

I could easily mimic one of the many unapproachable mobsters seen on TV and tell him to forget about it; however, I don't know which definition of "forget about it" I wish for him to keep. If they forget to remove me from this self-made blacklist, I'll ask if they want a piece of me and will not have Al Pacino's famous accent to accompany my threat. Whatever comes from me when I do see him, they will know their spectacular spectacle is now at its immediate end.

Jimmy Nix is not as slick as he thinks. Before the end of the night, I'll have all I desire, and he will foot the bill for his failure in concealing his identity longer than 24 hours. I smirk at my embellished fantasy of how the future will play out tonight. I envision more than I did just minutes ago, and I'm in awe at how an answer influences the way you see potential.

Thinking about the amount of time I'll spend at the bar, I know I'll need a shower before going. This will be a challenge. I'm not quite ready for a domestic affair, but I need a hygiene check. I remain in my parking space, contemplating the possibilities. It's pointless. I'll have to move to get where I wish to go.

I shift out of park and move towards the one direction I can't manipulate: home. If Jayden is there, I'll just have to wait until he leaves. For the second time in a very short while, I feel juvenile in my way of thinking. It's not enough to constitute a change in my plans. I drive home.

I pull into our parking deck slowly and cross my mind's imaginary fingers. In order to find out if he is home, I'll have to act as a stranger and ring my own apartment. I feel silly, but to my disbelief my luck is finally changing. After the second buzz, there is still no answer. He is not home, and I'll have the apartment to myself. Not knowing how long this window of opportunity will last, I rush twice as fast as normal.

Once inside, I call his name out of a conscious need to make sure he is not here. It's hard to believe that anything is actually going my way. When I'm sure that he is not going to surprise me, I take a shower in record time.

I bathe, dress, and return to my vehicle in under 20 minutes. I climb back inside, disheartened. Our apartment didn't have the welcoming scent of bacon, and having been in and out so quickly makes me yearn for the warmth and comfort that only home can provide.

I head back to the bar with mixed emotions. I long for two very different things. When I place my desires side by side, I can have either one, but not at the same time. My addiction speaks so loudly that it seems to drown out the argument.

My weakness sickens me. More than anything, I want to breathe free and live again, to have fellowship and brotherhood. As it sits now, I can do neither one successfully. I can't keep myself sober long enough to retain anything beneficial from any relationship I currently have. What I want is my past back, which is an impossible dream. I try to accept it, but it isn't as fulfilling as people promise.

At least when I use drugs, this empty guarantee seems easier to swallow. My life is nothing as I envisioned it growing up. I can remember as a toddler it was cowboys and Indians, and as an adolescent, G.I Joe. When I got to my teens it was Rambo, and as soon as I graduated from college, I was off to make a difference. Combat for a cause was the name of my game, and driving to this bar is the polar opposite of the righteousness of my former goals.

My addiction makes no sense to those who love me, and I can just barely keep my reasoning straight in my own mind. I'm doomed to keep repeating this vicious cycle until

I learn the maneuver that will outwit and defeat this ever-growing monster. The trouble is that I'm not role-playing in some game of fantasy. This is very much a real scenario with consequences that penetrate deeply.

Needing to avoid the sudden onset of depressing thoughts that surround my visit back home, I steer my thinking in another direction altogether. I focus on what is to come, and I'm back to wondering how this must be one of the most elaborate pranks I have ever seen. Jimmy's management of the details is impressive. His scheme is intricate, and this inspires me to force his disclosure of secrets regardless of his agreement.

I prepare an arsenal of questions that need answers. I don't plan to strong-arm my way to knowledge, but rather use the subtly of bourbon. My ego is dying to know why he is so confident that this trickery will succeed. It makes me wonder whether I'm unintentionally portraying a reputation of weakness to others.

Whatever his response is, I'll spin, of course, in the direction of humor so that his ability to brag squashes quickly. It kills me that I fell into his trap so willingly. I'm a fool. I doubt if I'll live this one down, but if I do, I'll not be so easily trusting or naïve the next time.

I still can't figure out how he got the girl in the café to play along, though. There is no way that he could have known I would go eat at that particular diner. I stop myself cold in the middle of thinking. In running through my mental cache of events, it dawns on me that the only way he could have known about the café was if he were having me tailed.

Instantly, I look in my rearview mirror to see who, if anyone, is following me. Paranoia is not a pretty thing, and as I peek behind me, I feel a little silly. I'll never be alone on these streets, no matter what time of day I choose to travel.

I sigh loudly at the probability of finding out prior to my arrival to the bar. I'll have to wait, even if it contradicts my policy of self-protection.

Despite my own personal principles of living lately, impressions on people are important. I cringe at how amusing I must have sounded to those at the table when I asked about the man hired to play the leading role in the practical joke. It's no wonder the bar roared with laughter. I conformed perfectly to the plot's design.

I wonder who all is involved and if it's any of the guys at the table from yesterday. I'll enjoy giving more than one friendly decking. Unfortunately, not all have relationships where physical violence is accepted as common affection. If I went in dishing out blows to their chops, they might not be so eager to call me off of the blacklist they so boldly invented.

I chuckle at the thought of how creative these junkies are. They really did have me going. Although I'm laughing, a certain portion of it, I'm afraid, is spite. I'm quite competitive by nature, and I hate to think that I fell short of the certain quick wit required to have not fallen victim in the first place.

I can't wait to expose Jimmy and sabotage his grand finale, whatever the plan may be. Even though we aren't best friends, I know why he believes us close enough to play the elaborate ruse. Jimmy and I have a habit of competing over everything. It's usually in good fun and lands us a pretty penny if we call our victories to begin with.

I walk around with such a tough guy image, and I'm not known for wearing my emotions on my sleeve. The bet is probably pretty steep and worth a lot of money. If he thinks he can win, he will pursue the challenge.

I realize I'll have to ease up on some of my aggression if I want to maintain this cool image I work so hard to achieve.

However the night plays out, I promise myself in this moment that I'll not give anyone the satisfaction of knowing how badly discouraged I am.

Although Jimmy really did win this one and has me in a way that I'm not proud of, I will not disclose it. I truly doubt that if he knew the extent of my torturous day, he would have developed such an evil plan. He has never brought harm to me and was actually the first one to vouch that I'm an alright guy to sell to.

On a few occasions, we have had deep conversations. He respects me when I find my limit in sharing and no longer wish to answer his questions. I actually think he might even have a point to much of this. After all, he taught me almost everything I know about street life.

As my nerve strengthens, I'm eager to find out his motives. I'm just around the corner and as ready as I can be. Shortly, I'll be singing a song of clever discovery for uncovering his masterful hoax prematurely, and I'll be back in good standing.

The humiliation of my wounded pride will mean nothing to me as long as I'm able to replenish my stash and get enough to forget this incident all together. This day needs to end so that my night may begin. With the darkness, I'll achieve cover and certain liberation from unwanted feelings that I'll do just about anything to rid myself of.

I park and make my way inside, passing the abrupt blare of music that hits me as soon as I walk in. I quickly scan the congested bar through the sounds that seem to conceal my friend. My senses drown in Steve Miller's Band and I scan the place to find the ultimate joker.

The bar is alive even before its famous happy hour. Every booth is full and every chair occupies someone. Even the corners are cause for traffic jams. It takes me longer to find Jimmy than normal. He is not at his usual table but shooting a game of pool. One thing is definite; the drought is over. These are the same people as the day before, but with new artificial pep in their step. A synthetic holiday is occurring, and I'm late in celebrating.

I consider the best plan of action, and decide to just walk right up to him and bust the operation wide open. After all, he always loves my direct approach.

Thinking that it has been quite some time since I have seen him this chipper, I lunge forward to catch the eight ball from sinking the corner pocket.

"Well, hello, my not-so-funny, long-lost pal who wants to send me to Sunday school. How's the old foot feeling? You know, the one you tried to kick in my face?" I speak as seriously as I can without cracking a smile.

"Well, what?" Jimmy's upper lip rises to blend fully into his mustache, but his demeanor is no more threatening than usual. "Dude, I had two bills riding on that shot. Thanks a lot."

I can see behind Jimmy that his competitor is already high fiving his own buddy at the unlikely turn of events. He practically prances his way over to claim the prize money. Jimmy just shakes his head and pays up, but not without challenging him to a rematch at a later date. As I watch him hand over the couple hundred dollars that I just cost him, I wait for him to question me. He looks me up and down. He shakes his head in sympathy at my appearance.

"I would say what's up with you, but I can see you're unhappy. Sit down and get yourself a beer. Waitress!" he shouts. "Bring my boy his usual."

I sit down and explode the second I do. "Dude, you have to tell me how you did it. I mean, this is the wildest thing I have seen yet. How on earth did you come up with such a crazy idea and please..." I hesitate, "tell me it's worth it?"

I hang my head as I shift from side to side, attempting to

get comfortable in my wooden seat. I open my eyes wide
for full understanding. His response assures me of nothing.
He just slumps forward, leaning into me with what seems
to be concern. I try and read his posture, even though we
are sitting. It does not reveal much. I expected to see more
confidence than this. I know pride, but what I see is a man
uncertain.

I disregard his lack of reaction and what his demeanor
speaks, and I carry on my conversation, even though he
looks at me this way. I plan to inquire for the rest of the
night, if I have to. I want answers, and I'll drag them out of
him.

"Jimmy, I'll admit, you had me going for a while there,
but I hate to break it to you, I figured it was you pretty early
on. For how much you put into it, I think I did a pretty good
job considering. All I want to know is how you pulled it off.
You must have had a whole crew working to help you on
this one."

The waitress interrupts my demands with my favorite
beer and places it near the only hand I have sitting on the
table. Jimmy throws a ten on her round serving tray, winks,
and expresses his desire for her to keep the change. As she
walks away, Jimmy's face returns to a tentative expression,
and I force my beer down my throat, trying again to appear
a little less anxious than I really am.

The bitterness of it stuns me. It tastes green, and I want
to spit it out. I force it down instead. I don't want to startle
Jimmy even more than he seems to be. If I only have what
I see before me as hope in finding what I seek, I'm afraid I
will not get my answers tonight. I wonder how lit he is.

I set the bottle down and take advantage of Jimmy's silence. I proceed in harassing him for the information I feel
he owes me.

"Okay. I get how you got me to go to the apartment, but

what I don't get is how you cleaned out the entire place when I was unconscious? I can see it vaguely with a whole lot of help, but the Bible? Come on, now. What are you trying to say?"

I smirk at the end of my question and again, Jimmy looks cross. I don't care. I need to get out what I'm harboring. With or without his feedback, I continue as intended.

"What I definitely can't figure out is how you knew I would talk to that waitress at the café. Well, let me back up. How did you know I would go to the café or that I would follow your guy's instructions to begin with? Were you following me? I better not be on candid camera somewhere, man, or I swear this will be your last night at the Night Bar."

I force another swallow of my wretched-tasting beer. This time I comment, "This is awful. I think my beer is stale."

I now have Jimmy's full attention. At this, he waves the waitress down. I kind of think he is grateful for the excuse to see her again. As she comes over, I look around to see who is here. I should not have to leave this bar at all tonight. Everything I want and need can be found through someone that is already here. This pleases me.

After she takes my beer away, I go ahead and ask if Jimmy will be so kind and remove my name from the list that causes me so many problems.

I wait patiently for his response and his agreement to revive my reputation, but instead Jimmy says, "What in the world are you talking about, man? What guy? What apartment? And who's this chick? She sounds hot."

Jimmy grins and is feeling better than average, I can tell. His mood is nonchalant, and it irritates me. Even though I'm compelled to shake him sober, his response gives me no indication that he is lying.

"Seriously, cut the crap, Jimmy. I'm in need here. Have you looked around? The entire bar is drenched."

With that, Jimmy now agrees. "That it is, my friend. So what's the problem with you?"

His response worries me. *Is he the responsible party or not?* I think to myself as I retort. "Jimmy, you're going to honestly sit here and keep all this up? I've busted you. Joke's over. I'm ready to handle my business, and you're interfering."

I now have his utmost full attention. He can easily see that I'm angry and that I'm blaming him. He looks at me, trying to clear his thinking enough to grasp the fact that I'm holding him personally responsible for my sobriety. Looking dumbfounded, I can see he is clearly not on the same page or even in the right book. His mind is just now beginning to register my complaints. He isn't getting why I'm not already set and joining him in a night of running the tables.

I observe every detail of his behavior in depth and see no deception. I begin to accept that he must truly be unaware of what is going on.

"Okay, slow down and hold up. First of all, I would never hate on you. Explain to me why you think I would even kick it like that with you? We're cool. I don't get in the way of others' happiness, man. That's not my style. I thought you knew that."

Jimmy's response makes me feel both better and worse at the same time. He is right. I do know that. We are as close of friends as a place like this allows.

From the beginning, I did not want to believe it was him, but I just assumed it was because he is the only one that I imagine could pull something like this off. After all, I know no one else who is linked to the local dealers like he is. My guts twist, and my alarm returns. Processing this new information, I panic. This means I'm still on the outs.

There is only one way to find out for sure. I plead for what he knows best: information.

"Jimmy, look, I'm sorry. I don't really know what's going on. I have had a really weird night. Look, I have two grand in my pocket. Who's best in the bar tonight?"

"Sammy is hot and so is Zeke. You can take your pick. If it was me, I would go with Zeke. He's usually better on that type of quantity," Jimmy answers, unhurt by all of my former accusations.

I'm now glad he has his head in the clouds and may not remember this tomorrow. I give him a half smile and take his advice with apprehension—not because it will prove to be no good, but because I fear that I'll be turned down.

Walking over to Zeke resembles traveling the dried up *Wadi*. There is never a time that you are not watching for the unexpected. The enemy is near, but you are not sure where. At any given moment, everything you know can turn threatening. Your feet can fall into a trap with each new step you take. Crossing a hidden IED is not an everyday occurrence but always possible. As I cross the room, I fear my stability for sure. I can't imagine life if the answer is no.

Approaching Zeke, he sees me before I reach him. With a quick signal, he passes on me. In the small swipe of a finger, he acknowledges my presence and denies it. I close my eyes and stop where I stand. My fear stems from a legitimate concern. My answer is no. As casually as possible, I try to look as though I have forgotten something at my table.

I turn around and my face is flush. I can feel the heat from my cheeks as I absorb what is happening to me. I'm really on the outs. I do not understand why. This is ridiculous. I can see if I did something to deserve this treatment but I haven't. I wonder why this is happening to me.

I return to my table a failure. Jimmy expresses surprise to see me return so quickly, and I read more confusion in his face. I can't help him. I'm lost, too. I decide to resort to what all junkies do and ask my friend to hook me up.

"I guess he is busy or not able to help me out right this sec," I say to him. "You think you could run ask Sammy real quick while I take a leak?"

Jimmy looks at me with curiosity. Never have I asked him to do me a favor when I'm capable of handling it myself. But with more courage than I have, he agrees and says, "No problem."

I tell him to look out for himself, and he quickly obliges. Not many can resist a couple hundred dollars in free dope, and since I just caused him a loss of this size, it's only fair. This is why we never really have a problem with one another. Our ledgers balance.

We simultaneously rise from the table and head in opposite directions. I move towards the infamous restroom where my nightmare began and Jimmy, to my last resort. As if I didn't know any better, I catch myself in prayer. *God, please don't leave me like this,* I pray. *Please help me just this once, and I'll confront my problems when I'm strong enough. Please.*

I close the restroom door behind me and lean into its frame. I plead silently with God as my fate is being decided outside. I've reached a new low in my life. How dare I petition God for help with something like this? I realize that I'm a sick, sick man. I stand in shame and try to catch my breath. I'm breathing too fast. I feel as though my chest will implode, and I think I'm hyperventilating. I have to calm down.

All of this confirms that my life is utter chaos. My turmoil is ruling me. There has got to be another way to live. I'm angry with myself, and I beat the door as if I could expel my problems through my fists. It doesn't work. A drop of sweat leaves my cheek, and it too fails to carry my problems with it. I guess if I could fight my way out of this, I would have been fixed long ago.

I rinse my face and dry my brow. I exit the restroom and upon returning, Jimmy is already back, with his hand resting under his chin. As soon as I see him, I can tell he is perplexed, and I know the answer is no. This means I'm in serious trouble. I sit down and stare at his conflicting expression. I think he rests his hand under his chin in order to pull the right words from his mouth; however, what sense can be made of this?

All he manages to say is, "Uh, I don't know how to tell you this, bro, but you're on the outs. I tried to find out why, but all he said is that it had to do with some deal you made or something."

Jimmy looks at me clueless and a question forms in his eyes. I had hopes that maybe he wouldn't use my name and just handle it under his own credit, but something must have changed his usual way. It's not like him to reveal a name or source. Thinking I might still have a shot if he will just say it's for himself, Jimmy continues.

"It's the strangest thing. I went over there for me, and it was like they just knew it was for you. I thought someone was eavesdropping, so I didn't deny it. When I admitted it, he told me that you were off limits and if I knew any better I would leave you alone myself before I find my own fate the same. Dude, I really don't know what happened to you last night, but whatever it is, you need to find out. This affects me if I want to know you, and I do."

This is the most sober I have seen him in all the time I've known him. I guess the threat of no drugs scares everyone who needs them and is certainly a road no one wants to go down. All I can manage is to bury my head in my hands. Within hours, I'll soon be the sweaty nightmare I was before I sought the strange man out.

Thinking about him turns my fear into rage. He is ruining my life. Who does he think he is to do such a thing? Who is he, to begin with? I wonder if he is a cop, wanting me off the streets? This can explain how he might know the dealers, but it doesn't explain why. I do not share and I pose no worthwhile threat to law enforcement. I'm only half present half of the time. I'm not dangerous to others. This seems outlandish, so I quickly discard the idea.

I free my mind to roam at will. I recall very little and not enough to help me. My head is still in my hands. I look through my fingers to see Jimmy gawking at me. I breathe deeply, remove my hands from my face, and rise from my seat. I'm marked, and it isn't fair to share my misfortune.

"I'm not sure either, man," I say, "but I plan to get to the bottom of this. Take care and look out for yourself. I'm gone. I'll let you know what I find out."

I throw a couple bills on the table for Jimmy, but as soon as they land he tells me to keep them, and good luck. I offer a weak smile of gratitude for his attempt to encourage me, then turn and walk away, jealous. This place is carefree, and I carry the weight of my fallen world.

CHAPTER SIX

Leaving the bar, I have no place to go. I don't even know where to start. I'm angry at everyone and everything. My life no longer has meaning or purpose. No one needs me or will use me, and, even worse, I'm the damage in need of repair. I'm not under the illusion that sobriety can't happen, just that it doesn't happen to a guy like me.

I have heard of others overcoming, but it's just far-fetched that I be a part of one of the many self-help units overflowing across America. I'm not cut out for continuous whining, and I'm past being spoon-fed the basics. With all I have experienced in life, I should be able to control something like this.

I hang my head as I walk to my truck. Who have I been kidding but myself? I don't know what's going to happen from this point forward, and it scares me. As soon as I recognize what I'm feeling, my training kicks in. I hear the echoes of drill sergeants far from their homeland.

The words of retired Colonel Wesley L. Fox rattle my brain as a part of an almost automatic reaction: "Fear is part of adventure, and learning to overcome fear is one of the benefits of embracing adventure."

I choose to act despite my fear. I stop and metaphorically pick myself up by my bootstraps. I may suffer, but so will this mystery man. I hardly believe this is the intended purpose of the value Colonel Fox taught us, but I'll use what I have left however I choose to use it. I harden my heart and bend it towards vengeance. Let the adventure begin.

The mystery man is going to pay for whatever it is he's doing. Almost instantly, I'm aware of the blood that circulates my face. Adrenaline begins to saturate my blood, and I'm ready to kill someone. If he thinks he can take me, let him try. I gun for my truck while muttering aloud, daring anyone to get in my way.

Once inside its black shell, I reach for the way of reckoning. I'll go to hell for this one, for sure. I pull my forty-five from the glove box and make sure it's fully loaded. The clip is empty, and so is the chamber. I slam my fist into the dash. Someone made sure that I'll not use my gun in anger.

"Stop screwing with me!" I yell but no one hears me.

Just one bullet is all I need to regain my sanity. I toss around the paperwork in my glove box from side to side, hoping that I can even the score. I find no extra ammunition. I grind my teeth into one another and close my eyes. I'm beyond humiliation, and I refuse to accept any more of what is happening. I make my mind up to retaliate. I have a new mission, and this guy needs to watch his back.

I take a deep breath and first consider that even though my opponent is weaker than me, he knows in general where I am. I figure it won't matter how much stronger I am if he can anticipate my attack. I embrace my fear and use it to heighten my awareness. I scan the lot before leaving my space. This man apparently knows me well enough to know where to hurt me. I'll have to find his weaknesses in order to get anywhere close enough to do any damage.

I pull out, heading nowhere specific, but I really need to be in a place of refuge to think. My mind shuffles ideas of how to ensue. Again, my beloved direct approach makes sense, but an opportunity will have to be made in order to deliver it.

I've never been one to jump at waiting, but in this case I believe it will be necessary. The mystery man isn't playing fair. All I want now is justice. He attacked me first, and since I feel dead, so will he.

I'm now ready to devour whatever gets in my way, and in thinking this, I notice something wedged between my wiper blade and the windshield.

"Great," I say. I have attracted the really annoying group of people who spread the news about their latest deals through the folding and inserting of recycled leaflets onto your private property.

"Stupid solicitors!" I hear my foul mood, and it gets worse when I realize I'm the only schmuck in the lot who got hit.

"Figures," I mumble. I slow to a stop, open the door, and snatch the folded flyer impeding my view. Refusing to litter, I throw it on the floorboard next to the equally unimportant leather book and head back in the direction of the apartment. I need to retrace my steps and see if, in my haste to get to the bank, I overlooked something important.

I arrive very quickly considering the time of day. It's amazing how fast I can accomplish a goal when I'm motivated. I step inside as a result of my request, and the overly mature doorman asks again for the reason behind my visit. I don't think he recognizes my face from this morning.

"Three-sixteen," I declare. He jots down the number and

routinely points to the elevators at the end of the hall. I'm confident that if someone comes knocking later asking questions, he will not be able to give an accurate description of anyone. This pleases me and will be helpful if the culprit of my misery comes back while I'm here and I act on impulse.

I head down the hall and squeeze onto the elevator, trying to blend in with those who are already waiting. I almost don't fit. It's evening and everyone obeys their body's alarm but me. The majority of the elevator empties before I reach the third floor. I get off with only two others. Fortunately, they enter their own apartments before I come to the one that brings me back for a second time in one day.

I look around and tap my backside. Even though there are no bullets, the sight of an automatic weapon will still stun most at first glance. It's in position and I'm ready. I don't expect anyone to be here, but I plan to be prepared if they are. I pop my neck in a circular motion and put my right hand on my pistol. With my left, I make a fist and give a courteous knock. No one answers.

I twist the knob to enter, but it's locked. I don't remember trying to protect the vacant apartment. I'm apprehensive, but when no one answers, I use force to pick the lock. I shove my gun back in my pants and pull out my wallet and pocket knife. With less time than it should take, I'm in. I shut the door quickly behind me before anyone observes the peculiar man breaking and entering apartment number 316.

I pull my gun immediately and point it directly into the void. The place is still empty. I scout each room to make sure there is no change from this morning. It's the same as I left it. The man is nowhere to be found. I lower my weapon to my side, along with my defenses.

I look around, still fuzzy about what all transpired here. The only thing I'm sure of is that what happened is significant. I wish I could remember more. The truth is that I was in the middle of a serious dope sickness, and in withdrawals that bad, nothing is clear. It almost feels like a bad high itself.

I take myself back, and I can see the man's face. When I try to hear his voice, there are only jumbled fragments. Every sound lingers, and my thoughts calculate incorrectly. My reaction time is slow and everything is hollow. Where the man goes in his speech, I can't follow. My mind protects itself with an imaginary wall that blocks anything other than an answer to its depleted chemistry.

I stand behind this barricade and emerge only when he speaks the language my addiction understands. As soon as I hear a remedy to my problem, I accept and am not concerned with the consequences of my choice. I agree and it's unfair from the beginning. I look back and see that I was handicapped last night, and this man took full advantage of my desperation and weakness.

I relax my stance and find a seat in one of the three available chairs the apartment offers. I look into the grooves of the worn oak table in front of me and follow the knots. Their peculiar shapes inspire me to pay attention to something else that is odd. There are only three chairs. I wonder where the fourth is and if the lack of chair is due to the fact that it's not needed.

It dawns on me that this man was not alone last night. I imagined on the way over that the man in the bar and the man in the apartment know each other, but I did not consider a third conspirator. I chastise myself for not seeing this possibility sooner, but there is no map or handy guide for trying to discover who is out to get you when you know as little as I do. It makes plenty of sense to use all the hands you can get. Clearing this place overnight is a mighty big job for one or even two.

I add this new option to what I know, which isn't much, but I'm still stuck on this stranger's motive. What can he possibly have against me? If I can understand why I'm his enemy, I may be able to predetermine his next step.

I imagine myself seated unconscious while all of the commotion of moving surrounds me. I accidentally recall my flashback from this morning, and I skip over this memory in order to keep focus. I try harder and concentrate on what they leave behind. The only concrete evidence besides the number of chairs is the book they left me: the Bible.

The Bible, it puzzles me still. Why is it their choice instead of an admission into rehab?

In the off-chance this guy believes he is helping, what will this book do for me? It's just words. He should at least pay a nurse to administer mood-stabilizing drugs during my detox, if he really wants to help me out.

People die during withdrawal from the narcotics I'm on. They are not just mentally addictive but physically. I catch myself getting angry and force myself to suppress this emotion. Right now I need to think, free of any deterrents that will cloud my judgment.

Being dope sick is worse than any sickness I have run across. It affects not only the body, but also the heart, soul, and mind. It's not enough to want to quit with just one or two of these things. You must be willing to surrender them all to the cause. Maybe that's what the man was getting at last night when he said I'll have to lose something.

I try my best to recall exactly what he said, but it's particularly vague. I stare into space with my eyes wide open. I allow gravity to pull my head back onto my shoulders, and I peer directly at the ceiling above. The stamps are random and without method, much like the facts I have to go on.

I relax my gaze and close my eyes. I feel the need to rest, but I'm undone. If I leave the clutch of this world, I chance further compromise. I can't risk it. I have to follow through with the tiny clues I've collected.

I think about the small, leather book left for me to find. Having the Bible in my vehicle reminds me of my grandmother. She always took hers with her everywhere she went. It was not important where she was going, just that she had this book of wisdom with her. It's probably still by her side today, even though she has passed away. Hers was so cluttered with markings that you literally had to strain your eyes in order to see past the highlights and smeared ink to read the words hidden behind them. Hopefully, whoever owned the Bible that rests in my truck left a personal mark of their own. Any notations will be helpful.

With this thought, I get up and head to the door. I need to reexamine the Bible. I purposely leave the place unlocked just in case I need to return again. I head back to the parking deck in a hurry. I find my truck much easier this time. I hop in and lock the doors. I'm starting to feel sketchy and vulnerable already. My adrenaline is not gassing me like it was earlier. I function now on the energy I have left in reserve, but it will not last long.

What keeps me motivated is knowing what tomorrow will be like if I don't find answers today. The later it gets, the more tired I feel. I press on and lean over the seat once more. I pull the Bible into clear view. I place it in my lap and open it. The print is tiny, and I have to squint.

I look up and around. The problem isn't the small type but the lack of light. It's getting dark outside. The cover of night will be helpful to conceal my identity, but I can't hunt until I have more facts to go on. I click the dome light overhead. The glow creates enough luminosity to search the worn-out book.

I read the opening page. Within the first paragraph, it declares itself as a bestseller where hope, joy, peace, and the answers to life can be found. It claims that it's truth and that this testament contains the very words of God. I almost close the book to avoid conflicting feelings, but I know that if I do I'll forfeit any direction it may possibly give. Grudgingly, I continue to skim through its pages for any indications that might help me.

I skip around and over a few books in between. I pay more attention to how thin the pages are than what is actually on them. This Bible has seen better days. It almost qualifies as trash, and if it does not serve the purpose I intend it to, it will be.

I thumb through with my right hand while my left is on its spine. I support the delicate pages from falling apart. I imagine that whoever owns this is definitely interested in the formula for salvation. I sigh. My own lack of redemption irritates me. Not only is life not progressing according to plan, but neither is this evening.

The book seems to be graffiti-free. I continue my search, becoming more and more irritated with each passing page. I slow down and attempt a more thorough method. I hardly keep the patient pace. The more I search, the more aggravation I feel. I see nothing jumping out to grab my attention and point the way to my mark. I feel the need to end my search early, but just as quickly as the thought enters my mind, I come across three lines that are underlined.

A tiny bit of excitement encompasses me and I lean in to read the words meant for me. Whatever they say will help me know my aggressor better.

Beloved, never avenge yourselves, but leave it to the wrath of God, for it is written, "Vengeance is mine, I will repay, says the Lord." (Romans 12:19, ESV)

My gut coils a knot around my fear, and I immediately throw the book to my side and begin looking for something suspicious. There has to be a wire that doesn't belong. I feel around inside the vents, paying extra attention to which direction they face. They are clean. I check the creases in the liner above my head and find nothing. I run my hands beneath the edges of my seat and run across the wrapper of an old candy bar and no more. I lift the mats off the floorboard and pat down the underside of my dash. I do not find the device I seek, but I know he is watching.

I leap from my truck and begin a quick search of the parking lot. Car by car, both front seat and back, I search for anyone who is looking at me. I see no sign of him or a camera, but he has to be here. There is no way this guy is planning all this in advance. I head back to my truck, more cautious than before.

As anxious as I am about the whole thing, I'm starting to realize that I'm not dealing with an amateur and that surprise is useless. This guy is good and definitely a pro of some sort. I'll give him the credit, but, unlike him, I will have my vengeance.

I return to my vehicle and back to my seat to continue my search for answers. This time with more zeal for the project, I pay closer attention. This man is trying to rattle me, and we both know that toying with people's emotions is a dangerous game.

I start again back at the beginning. I pass the page with the very large promises and search for any penned names or addresses left for recall. There is nothing to find. I hope, at the very least, to locate his church's name or any group he has affiliation with, but I'm not so lucky. The previous owner leaves no record of baptisms or wedding dates. He doesn't record his family deaths or mention the birth of anyone new. This is puzzling.

"Why leave me this, then? What do you want me to know?" I ask the book, even though it doesn't speak.

I check the publisher on the off-chance it's local. It's not and even if it is, it's the most popular book in the world. They probably mass print this exact edition and pass it out on every street corner during evangelism week.

There is nothing left to find. I'm unsuccessful and near the end of my search. I come to its final pages and am ready to move on. Right before I close the back cover, I catch a glimpse of a small handwritten note next to the inside bottom corner. It's written very neatly in black ink. All the words are uppercase, so I assume the penmanship is a man's.

Dear Sweetheart,

If you are reading this, I never returned to you. I'm sorry, my darling. My intention was never to abandon you. You must feel that I have left you without hope or a way to move forward. But that just isn't the case. I may not be there to walk you to school, but if you carry this book, you will know where I am and that I, too, care about your learning. Many things may happen over the course of your life, things that you may never understand, but handle them always and know God is watching.

If your Uncle Dan makes it home before me, give him this book and tell him Ductus Exemplo. He will understand. Only do not pass it on until after you have completed reading it from cover to cover. The true message I share with you both is revealed in all of its pages.

I love you.

There is no name declaring ownership of the words, but I know he is a Marine, probably an officer. It's also likely that this Uncle Dan is an officer too, or at least affiliated enough with them to know what this Latin phrase means.

Things are taking an interesting turn, but reading the missive brings back personal memories of my own. Jotting down farewells are never easy. I did it four times and all four times were difficult. There are no words to console the grieving when their loved ones are snatched from them prematurely. Even if you explain that it's your choice to go, you leave the door open for them to blame you for not staying. It's hard for many to understand that we have to go for more than just the obvious reasons.

I read the letter over again once more. I'm glad that my letters were to my mom and not to a wife or, worse yet, a child like this. Moms just need to hear that they did a good job of raising you and that no matter how it all turns out, you would make this bold choice again. I cannot imagine sitting down and writing a wife one last love poem or asking a baby girl to forgive me for missing her high school prom. If I had a family of my own, I'm afraid the right words would be much more difficult to find.

Cot thoughts buzz in my ear. I can hear my brothers' stories from here. "My wife just had our son. He's healthy and has a ton of hair. I can't believe I'm missing it." "My son made All-Star for the first time, guys. He's been playing ball for five years. He has worked so hard. I can't believe I'm missing it." "My brother broke his arm in the end zone playing college football last week. He scored the game-winning touchdown, though. I can't believe I missed it." "Today was my twins' first day of kindergarten. My wife says they had a blast. That they came home and went straight to the closet to pick out what they wanted to wear tomorrow. She says they think they're grown up now. I can't believe I missed it."

I hear the stories that kept us alive, but I also hear the ones that killed us. "My mom and dad are getting a divorce after twenty-five years of marriage. I don't know how they can just quit like that after being together so long." "My wife is sleeping with one of my friends. She wants a divorce first thing when I get home." "My niece has cancer. The treatments aren't working, and they don't really expect her to live another year. My sister is devastated."

It doesn't matter if you're standing post or on guard watch, the news of a death of someone close to you is always the worst. "My pops died this afternoon. They think he had a massive heart attack. He was only fifty-five. I don't know how my mom is going to get through this."

Death is permanent, and we are fragile. Hearing this Marine's final thoughts move me, but in what direction I'm not sure. Like my comrades back in Iraq, this man's words will linger.

I close the Bible with more respect for the leather book than I had just moments ago. Contrary to my earlier assessment, it's not waste or garbage to toss. I'm uncertain why the Bible is separated from its owner and how it found its way to me, but there is a reason.

I think about the meaning of the words *Ductus Exemplo*. It's the motto Marine officers cling to. It means to lead by example. With this new information, I'm truly stumped. I don't know what to think, and for my overly analytical self, this is unusual. I don't even have a theory. It seems I'm being taunted by the final words and thoughts of a dead Marine and his Bible.

There is no logic to what is happening. I glance through the windshield and look around again for something out of sorts. There is nothing to see but nightfall, and it's approaching quickly.

I consider my plans for the night. I'm already beginning to ache. I think of Jayden, and, even though I'm not capable of debating, I wonder what he must be thinking right now. I know this isn't easy for him, but I can't help him understand. I don't have the words or the energy to try and explain it to him. Shame dominates me, and what I am is embarrassing. Out of respect, I pull out my phone and compose a short text message to ease his mind.

"Out of town to think. Don't expect me for a couple of days." I send the brief excuse and nothing more.

I'm not sure what his response will be, but Jayden is usually very good at giving me the space I need. I hope there is no debate. I stare at my phone. I know gawking at it will not make him answer any sooner, but I do it anyway.

As I wait, I consider the possibility that I'm being a bit selfish in expecting such a quick response. I have been avoiding him for weeks now, and here I am, hoping he will hurry up and confirm that he received my message. I start to evaluate the type of person I'm becoming, but before I'm forced to acquire patience, Jayden responds and his answer is simple: "Be careful."

I read his reply and am reminded why I'm so fond of him. He never jumps to negative conclusions or worries over spilled milk. He is the best friend anyone can ever ask for, and I'm more often than not a jerk undeserving of his loyalty.

I sense a bit of relief having postponed my face-to-face with him. My stomach growls, but again I neglect the simple task of feeding myself. I decide that it's better to force myself to eat now rather than in between hurlings later.

I start my truck. Fast food and posting up at the empty apartment is my short-term goal. I'm not bonding with the atmosphere, but the isolation it offers will allow me the time I need to think. I turn my truck back off. I can get a cold cut, pickle, and chips right down the street without having to drive. I'll grab a few extra waters on the way and save an hour.

I'm not sure if this is a wise choice. I pull my key from the ignition, and I'm still appreciative of the fact that I don't have to converse with anyone. Unless the stranger returns to the apartment, I'll be alone and can search through virtual reality in peace. For the time being, research is appropriate, and I'm curious to know what can be learned through posts and conversation.

I get out of my truck and begin to collect all that is needed. I check the items on my mental list one by one: dinner, drinks, Bismuth, Acetaminophen, my laptop, and the Bible. I stand there to make sure I don't leave anything important. I can't afford to waste energy on useless returns due to negligence or poor planning.

I stand and shove the remaining items that I'll use in my defense into my pockets. They start to bulge, and the weight loss over the course of the last few weeks proves helpful for the first time.

In my left pocket is a knife, garbage ties, a mini Maglite, a lighter, and keys, and in my right is my gun. My back left pocket contains my wallet, and my back right is empty but pressing hard against my cheek. I'm thankful my phone has its own holster on the outside of all this, and with just one more thing, I think I'm ready.

I reach into the back of my truck for my spur-of-the-moment, always-packed, black duffel bag that Jayden and I keep ready in case we ever want to road trip the weekend. It contains everything we need for a couple days in the wilderness.

Now feeling more prepared, I buy my food and make my way to 316. Once inside, I lock the door and set down my supplies. I'm hungry and don't waste time unwrapping my entire sandwich. I pull down the sleeve and shovel the salami and Swiss into my mouth and finish before my laptop is up and running. It's satisfying; I wish I had ordered two.

I wipe my mouth and sit down at the table. I open my bag of chips and finish an entire 20-once water in just a few swallows. I must be getting dehydrated. I still feel thirsty. I grab another water and log on to the internet using wireless access.

I enter the address of a local military forum that I used to visit when I first moved to New York. Sometimes there is unusual chatter, and if you listen closely, you can find out the latest gossip both here and abroad. In a way, signing on still excites me. I miss knowing more than civilians.

I enter my username and password. Once in, the filters arc off. Marines and soldiers are pouring over the latest controversy, and bickering is a nice way of putting it. It's not unusual to hear opposing views, but whatever the topic is today, it has this local web community heated. I grin. I'm reminded that many of us are hot-headed and speak before we think.

I scan the posts and comments, skipping very little. I'm looking for any information concerning a deceased Marine and his missing Bible. So far, I see nothing relevant. What I do see reminds me that knowledge is simply necessary.

I listen to what they say is happening overseas. It makes the war seem a sensible and just response. Not knowing my nemesis, his motives, or his goals makes this search somewhat blind, and, of course, completely unwarranted. I'm painfully aware that I'm extremely short of critical information on this guy. If I plan to learn his methodology at all, I'm going to need more than what I have to go on.

I give the air a big pirate's "Argh" like it can intimidate the computer into surrendering these facts. I'm stupid. I'm stupid for getting myself into such a mess, and I'm stupid for not being able to get out of it. I kick myself and then the table beneath me. Nothing happens. I guess I'm hoping to shake loose an answer I have yet to think of. It's frustrating trying to figure out how a stranger's mind works.

I stare at the screen, waiting for something to jump out and point the way to a real resolution. It doesn't so I decide to check my email while I wait for a plan to manifest itself. My inbox is flooded with over 100 emails, easy. This is my consequence for disappearing.

The majority looks to be ads, but I do see a few from family and friends. I delete the junk mail to make room for what is more important. One by one, I trash the items of insignificance, and I stop and read a few in between. So far, Jacob requests a trip to his neck of the woods, and Mom is checking to see why I haven't called lately. I look at the dates on each of these messages and see that they were sent over a month ago.

Again, it's clear. I'll not receive an award this year for being the best at anything. I'm no number one son or number one cousin or friend while I'm making accusations against myself. I sigh and move on.

I open a few advertisements from local gun retailers, and, of course, it temporarily takes my mind off the declaration I just made. Unfortunately, the excitement lasts for only a second, and I'm already bored. I delete them and continue.

The next email I come to is actually from today. I reread the sender's name, trying to recall who it is. It only takes twice, and I feel excitement again. It's from Steven Briggs. The subject reads: "Greetings." Steven and I go all the way back to Parris Island and Basics. I'm not sure where Steven is stationed now, but I envy him, wherever it is.

I open the email only to be welcomed by a symptom of withdrawal first. My stomach turns and sounds the alarm that my larger problem is now beginning. Instead of waiting until it's uncontrollable like the market, I down some Bismuth and hope to avoid it. I wage that symptom management is a great idea and go ahead and take the Acetaminophen, too.

I feel the warning in my stomach. I'm not looking forward to this again.

"God, why do I do this stupid stuff?" I ask the question before I realize who I address it to. I'm in shock, and I'm sure He is, too.

I look down at my watch, trying to ignore what I just asked. I try and estimate the time I have before the storm really hits. In just a short while, I'll be at a full 24 hours without substance, and I already want to die just thinking about it. These feelings are aggravating, and imagining my near future is overwhelming.

I pull my phone from my hip. In desperation, I try again and see if I may have overlooked someone who can help. I scroll through the assorted numbers and contacts. I'm not missing anyone. They are all related to each other in some way or another. Even if they don't know each other, their sources are the same.

I fight to find someone or something that will cooperate. I throw my hand into the air out of frustration and ball my fists, ready to fight the first thing that presents itself to me. I let out a huge sigh and try to breathe deeply. There is nothing to retaliate against.

I notice the pang in my side beginning to ease. My self-medicating is working. I take advantage of the relief and refocus my attention on the words in front of me. Steven is brief.

Hey, man. I haven't talked to you in awhile. I hope life is treating you good. Get back with me, would you? I have a lot to catch you up on. Steven

The note isn't difficult, but I catch myself already typing a vague response, avoiding anything personal. My superficial reply explains in one short run-on sentence that I'm good, extremely busy with life, and that all is well. I send it before I can think more deeply about it.

As soon as I do, I regret it. Steven is a good guy with no family that I know of. If I'm not mistaken, the main reason for his joining the Marines to begin with was to have brothers, and here I am being distant to an already lonely guy.

I realize I'm a jerk for the second time today and that I am, among other things, shallow. I lower my head. It's hard to keep up the pretense in my mind that I'm a good guy. As if I didn't already have enough on my plate, dealing with my character defects is not on my agenda.

I stare at my screen. It shows a confirmation of mail sent. I use my mouse to click on the compose button. Steven deserves more from me. I begin typing another letter. I'm not sure yet whether I'll be amending or elaborating on the existing. My plan is to just type and see what comes out.

As I do, my computer chimes, alerting me of new mail in my inbox. It's a response from Steven already. He must be sitting at his computer now. I wonder what he is up to and doing this time of night or day, wherever he is. I open his response more eagerly than before, genuinely interested in what he has to say.

Good to hear back from you so quickly. It doesn't surprise me you're doing good. I figured you and Jayden were out sightseeing the world and it would be later before sooner that I got up with you. I was wondering, if I made my way to New York, do you think you could put me up for a few weeks until I figure out what I want to do? I got caught in the middle and lost the use of my right arm. It's still attached, but I have no feeling and it doesn't do what I tell it.

The letter ends just as it starts, right in the middle of a conversation. I cringe reading the words of another Marine who is suffering. In front of me is something that truly merits compassion. He would not have asked if he had another place to go.

Without further thinking, I approve his request with conviction. The thought of having one of my brothers out there all alone makes this decision easy. I can't imagine what my life would look like without Jayden's company. I'm willing to bet my issue is more common than people think.

Disappointment is tough, and being alone is even worse.

Together they equal disaster. If I can help it, I won't risk another one ending up like me. I'll be Steven's family even if I offer nothing more than a warm place to stay and good food to eat. He will know in the end he is always welcome. I have his six just as Jayden has mine.

I finish the letter without consulting Jayden. I don't have to worry if it will be okay with him. They know each other well, and Jayden always says, "The more the merrier." Jacob will enjoy the new addition, too, since they are one *compadre* down without me hanging around. Three increases the betting pot, and he truly is a jarhead fan.

My house is your house, man. Come on. These are the final words of my response, and I click the send button again. It's been a long time since I've felt sorrow for anyone other than myself. I realize with my invitation to stay as long as he likes that I'll be found out in all that I am. At this point, it doesn't really matter. My motive for offering is based more on my own experience than what he says in his request. Alone is where I sit. I don't want this for him.

In my experience, being lonesome is one of the more common reasons people get wasted. People can find this burden with or without help, but once here, everyone wants out. The walls that line my heart are thick, and even though I have others around, I seclude myself until I no longer know how to verbalize to others what it is I feel.

If I could go back, I would in an instant. I don't know in words how to describe the disaster of my heart, and as I take each new pill the need to say anything disappears all together. I can't let him end up like me. He has an opportunity to know something much different.

Dude, I can't tell you what this means to me. I leave here in a week or so and will head your way. I don't know what to say but thank you!

His appreciation comes quickly and my troubles increase.

Having Steven see me this way will probably tear him up like it does Jayden. None of us wants to turn out this way. Half of our fathers who went to Vietnam did, and we swore we would never take the same path. But here I am just as lost and overtaken by this world.

All this time, I have not seriously considered trying to kick this habit for good, but it has now become a matter worthy of sincere attention. What if here and now is the time to start over? *Can I do it?* I ask myself this question, and I wait to hear myself respond. My soul is not naturally willing. I have no hope in storage, and my energy is depleted. Defeat is certain.

My cell phone startles me and interrupts my doubtful thinking. The ringtone for my mother is distinct, and I don't need to check the number to know it's her. My lack of response to her many emails is surely the reason for her call now, but I know if I ignore her she will just call Jayden to check up on me, and that scares me worse than lying to her. I have no choice but to answer.

"Hello?" I say.

My mind drifts immediately to Jayden's great ability to win the affection of parental figures. He is just plain sweet in dealing with them, and I wish I could tap in to his power right now and calm my mom's spirit. She immediately expresses her deep concern for my lack of communication, and I can think of no excuse for her yet.

"Yes, Mom, Jayden and I do plan to come for Thanksgiving, and I'm sorry I haven't called sooner."

It's amazing how a promised visit changes her tone. I can hear the excitement in her voice grow, and I agree that I'm also excited. "Yes, Mom. That's great. I can't wait."

With this statement, I'm now officially dishonest. I'm in no way thrilled to show myself as I am. It will actually cause problems on one of my mom's favorite holidays. As if I'm not already sick from withdrawals, I feel sick agreeing to this.

My mom asks about Jacob. I realize that I need to RSVP one more and include Steven. If I remember correctly, he grew up in foster care and Thanksgivings are not so happy. He will be thrilled to realize the military did give him the family he always wanted after all. I just hope he can forgive my current state.

"Mom, if you don't mind, I want to bring one more. A buddy of mine named Steven will be staying with us for awhile, and he doesn't have any family to spend it with. Is that alright?"

I wait only a split second to hear her agree, and a new joy manages to erase the fears she originally called with, or so it sounds. I secretly hope this is enough to keep her off my back for a couple of days.

We exchange a few details, and I hang up by sending my love through the sound of a kiss that confirms all is well. I begin to hate my mouth. Lately, it keeps me in constant trouble. I know that it's anatomically necessary for it to be constantly working, but if I could I would force this muscle to atrophy. I'm making promises I can't keep. Again I begin to consider life without an anchor. I tilt my head back in my chair and ponder life a different way.

I don't like what I see. My imagination creates a place where I'm absent in conscious form. One moment I'm in the apartment alone with only myself for company, and the next I'm in the midst of open fire across the streets of New York. Only New York looks more like Colorado Springs, and the weather is hot like Iraq in midsummer.

I'm running toward Quantico, Virginia, as if it's just a mile down the road. This makes no sense. I aim to break in and steal base files on all former military personnel with the first name Dan, but my legs aren't moving fast enough to get me there in time. This isn't right. In no case would I try something so stupid. I'm dreaming. I can't wake myself up.

My mind weaves its own experience in with the gentle braids made up of my desires and fears, and I can't understand the twisted reality. Things aren't as they seem, nor do objects move at the same pace. I'm going nowhere fast. My feet move at warp jelly speed, and the harder I fight to get them working appropriately, the more infected I become with this travesty.

I fight anyway. Just as I get close to a breakthrough and think I can force the motion, I fall into the backseat of my Grandfather Rex's four-door Plymouth. It smells like stale coffee, cheap after shave, and fast food. We pull in to the drive-in theater, and I'm eager to watch *E.T.* for the fifth time. I settle in, and, as I do, Grandpa Rex informs me that I have to sign the ticket before I can watch the program.

I'm not too young to sign my own name, but he hands me a packet of ketchup, and as odd as it is, I know what to do with it. I open the package and sign the ticket with what represents my life in blood. He accepts and with this he turns around and hands me something wrapped in a brown paper bag. I begin opening it, and something pokes into my backside. The pain wins out over the urgency of my task, and I choose to rectify this problem first.

My attention transfers from the sack to my seat, and I wake up feeling as though I have grown roots to the chair I fell asleep in. I'm sore and the apartment is dark. All I can see are the blinking lights on my electronic devices.

I must have been out for hours. I extend my legs, trying to ditch the sleep that holds me temporarily captive. I'm stiff and feel worse than I did before I dozed off. I check my watch again. My hope to have slept a day away fades. It has only been an hour.

Sobriety is already offering more time than I'm used to. I tap my keyboard for more light. I close my eyes at the sudden burst, but there is no hope in returning to my dreams. My mind is awake, even though my body is not.

I yawn and force myself to stand. The popping of my joints tells me I'm old before my time. My injuries ache. I look around and make sure nothing has been disturbed while I slept. Nothing has.

I walk around stiffly at first but quickly incorporate a pace in the shape of circles. I shift my weight back and forth between my two legs, and this alternation doesn't clear my head like it usually does. I know I want to try, but I don't know where to start. I wrestle with the choices in my mind: Continue using, get sober, continue using, get sober, continue using, get sober.

The ritualistic petal-picking doesn't tell me how all of this will end. I'm going to have to make a decision and stick to it, whatever it may be. It has to be fully intentional, and once I decide, I must be deliberate in every action.

I keep pacing. It's a decision I can't avoid. If I choose sobriety, I'm standing on the brink of a possible doorway to life. If I choose vengeance and drugs, my hovering is over an entry way to continual chains. The answer is clear just horribly hard to submit to. The promise of life comes with feelings, pain, disappointment, and shame.

The list reflects the consequences for oblivion, but in this desensitized realm I'm unaware that this is what I'm suffering. I see this clearly now and feel foolish. Drugs do not take away my issues; they just conceal them. I dance from side to side, seeing struggles with both choices.

The second I arrive at a decision in my mind, the opposing side sweeps in to argue its case. One is persuasive while the other manipulative. One tells me I have a choice, and the other dictates orders. I don't know why I make this so hard. *Just agree to one Casey,* I think. I patronize myself in hopes that the audible order will force a decision.

"This is silly. I want to live."

I decide on impulse, and it throws me for a loop to hear my own voice so emphatic. I wait to hear myself recant, but I don't and it's official. I will live my life in a sober mind. I don't know how or exactly what to do at this point. I look around for answers and stop when I see the leather book sitting on the floor next to my duffel bag, waiting so patiently to be read. I consider the words of the dead Marine concerning hope, and I pick up the book to make sure I remember them correctly.

"You must feel that I have left you without hope or a way to move forward. But that just isn't the case ... The true message I share with you both is revealed in all of its pages."

What is truth? I wonder and even though I may later declare the whole endeavor pointless, I decide to attempt to find out what the message means. I back up and reread the entire letter again. I'm sure now. Whatever the news is, this man felt it necessary to pass it on in his final words. There must be something to it.

I rub the cover of the used book, as I'm certain others have done before me. I imagine they really want to know, too. They would have to. The number of pages alone will stop the average Joe from its pursuit. I look to see just how many, out of curiosity, and I immediately regret it.

"Good Lord, nine-hundred and six. Really? Come on, now. You could have made this a little easier."

I shake my head in rebellion, but his instructions are simple: read it cover to cover. I huff, but it doesn't change a thing. The book continues to wait for my companionship.

"It better be like magic," I say to the book, and my threat proves that age does not mandate maturity.

My imagination carries me away. In my fantasy, I see a changed life, one filled with joy and many pleasantries. It seems possible. The reach is far, but I believe it's doable. For the first time, I have a real urge to break open the Bible and read with expectancy. I catch myself almost smiling, and just as I crack it open and accept its invitation of hope, my phone rings.

It distracts me from these feelings, and I'm cross—not at the disruption but in how flighty my thinking is. One second I'm willing to trust someone who knows a better way, and the next I hope it's someone calling who can get me pills. As quickly as I hope in one, I hope in the other. I'm pathetically weak-minded.

My aggravation and all it represents gets to me, and I take my phone and hurl it against the apartment wall without discovering who is calling. I don't care. It breaks into pieces, and I'm hardly satisfied. I'll never be successful with so many distractions. I leave the phone where it lies.

I'm discouraged before I even begin. My indecisive behavior cripples me. It's pushing me farther and farther away from the momentum I need to get started. If I plan to accomplish my goal, I'll need a real miracle of divine intervention. I don't know exactly what to do, but I need help. I can't do this by myself.

I complain as an unusual thought crosses my mind. I could do like many others and pray. I'm not sure how effective the prayers of a broken man can be to a God that I'm not positive cares, but I think it's worth a try. At the very least I'm sincere, and if He is truly aware of everything, He knows this. If God chooses to answer based on merit alone, I'm doomed anyway.

I leave the dining area and head back to the bedroom with the sole mattress. I lie down and roll into a fetal position. I don't know what it looks like to pray in faith, but it feels natural to position myself in honesty.

"God," I call for His attention, and I don't know why I

can't bring forth more words. Somehow I feel unworthy to even speak His name and this is a phenomenon I'm not familiar with. I have cursed and blamed God many times, and the words came freely. Now my desire is to plead with Him for aid, and I'm silent.

I roll onto my back and spread my arms and legs to their maximum. I plaster my eyes on the ceiling of this very dark room and stare so hard into the darkness that it looks like it could take form if it so chose.

"Please, God," I try again. "Help me fight myself."

The ceiling does not answer back, and I wonder if it's too late for me. Tomorrow I'll be in a battle with my own flesh whether He helps me or not, and I really am too weak to tough it. I won't blame Him if He doesn't show up. I don't deserve His assistance. After all, I did do this to myself.

I close my eyes and feel vulnerable again. My wit begins to shuffle different ideas through my mind, and I see no reason to restrain the images. Any dream is better than what I face when I wake up.

CHAPTER SEVEN

The fight is underway. I'm lying on the bathroom floor with a towel by my side and a book as my pillow. My head clings to my shoulders only because it's forced here by creation. I'm spinning and the light of day brings nothing but a consistent barrage of symptoms, further proving my problems. The floor is invitingly cold and offers me the only relief I have experienced so far.

I've been this way for at least an hour now. When I woke up, I thought I would never make it to the bathroom in time. I didn't realize then that I would not be able to return to slumber. This is the epitome of dumb, if I have ever seen it before, and my hatred for drugs grows every time I hurl.

My dehydration forced me out of the bathroom only once, and now I just stare at the bottle that looks better than it is. Every time I try and drink it, I just throw up again. I realize how dangerous this all is and consider throwing myself at the mercy of a hospital, but I doubt I could even make it there if I tried. I'm stuck in this apartment and its provision of cool tile.

I ache all over and as the minutes pass it's getting worse. Every wound reminds me of its presence and between the foulness of uncontrollable urges and the pain, I want to quit even though it's not an option.

Earlier when I brought the Bible into the bathroom with me, I had hopes of using it for inspiration, only I cannot focus even to read its pages. Right now it simply serves as something besides the ground to prop my head against so that it isn't equal with the floor beneath me. Ironically, the Word of God is helping regardless of my inability to understand it.

Time is slow if you watch it. I consider removing my watch. I lie here, and it seems like it takes a whole day for an hour to pass, but I know this is just my perception. I've been told the pace of my detox depends on how addicted I am and to what, but if money can end my misery in a shorter timeframe, I swear there is no dime I will not spend.

I hold the position most likely not to hurt and discard the notion that money can fix this. I'm alone with the exception of the words of God, and this is apparently how it's supposed to go for me or I wouldn't find comfort in the fact that they sit with me. They seem overly patient and wait without judgment of my inability to retain them at this moment. It's unexplainable, but I'm developing a fondness for them before I have even read them.

I consider myself independent. I can muscle my way through any tough problem. No amount of physical strength I have comes close to equally matching the evil I'm facing. Every time I think I can challenge it, I sit up and within seconds return to my place of humility by the Bible's side. It's as though there is a message in this and the point is, don't go far. But I'm in no shape to understand anything deeply. I just want help.

I want to argue with someone, and I don't know why. I want to lash out, but I have no energy. I want to prove something, but I have no point.

"God!" I yell. "What do you want from me?!"

My scream is loud enough that every neighbor can hear. I hope they haven't. I don't wish to be a spectacle tonight. I list the reasons why I can't start reading the book now, and among the top five are excuses that start with, "I can't." When I honestly stack the legitimate ones before me they aren't even high enough to surpass the height I lay. I have no good reason for not trying but that I am stubborn and hardheaded. I know my instructions and they are simple but I am avoiding following them. Even worse, I am still blaming my situation on why I can't move forward. It is pathetic. In not following the instructions, I hurt me. I hate when facts are blunt and declare my stupidity so easily.

I lift my head and remove the inanimate object that forces my compliance. I replace the book with my towel and I open it to its beginning. The book I start with is called Genesis and within a very short time I discover that I am incredibly misinformed. I am not ultimately to blame for my current situation and that it is all Adam's fault. I immediately perk up and am delighted to blame another for my situation. From this moment on, I decide to read with an open mind.

Chapter after chapter I am intrigued by what the Bible reveals and as I enter the very last chapter of the first book, I notice that an incredible amount of time has passed since I started reading. Something more amazing is that I did this without the want or need to excuse myself.

It is exciting and confusing at the same time. The God I manifest is nothing like the one I read about. This God deserves our fear and he acts like a real owner. It is remarkable that I am only just now discovering this.

I close out the end of the book and read about a man who

overcomes incredible circumstances that are not even a result of his own making. I reflect and of course feel pretty lame having whined so intently over my own. I review the ancient stories in my mind and I come to one very logical question that if I don't establish the answer to now will result in my doubting of the Bible's authenticity later. Is this God indeed the rightful creator and maker of all things I see and are these his words? If I answer no then the Bible carries absolutely no weight at all but if I answer yes than I am stumbling over the greatest manual ever written.

I have never read another book that stirs me as this one. My suspicion is that it is in fact the truth but if this is the case, many more questions arise that I need answers to. Inspiration to continue reading grows from somewhere within me but I am troubled by the whole consequence of sin theology. If I can technically blame Adam for starting it all and get away with it then what is the point of writing the rest of the Bible? Apparently, I am premature in believing there is no need for something to redeem me. After all, Adam is not laying here on this floor now, I am. The fact that I am born into a fallen world is secondary. I make the choices I suffer for, no one else, me, and me alone.

This makes me sick to my stomach again but in a different way than what I have been experiencing. My reaction is due to a realization of a need that is not being met in my life. I am unsure how to rectify this problem and give myself a few minutes to try and come up with a workable solution. Unfortunately, in my own abilities, I have no formula to an equation of emptiness.

I hold the Bible to my chest and try making a final decision about its credit and what my next direction will be. Before I can move forward, I must determine if I do, in fact, hold the words of God in my hands.

From within the pit of me, I immediately feel unworthy,

and I know my answer. I let go of all that hinders me and from the farthest corner of heart, my pride falls. I cry. I cry like I've never cried before. Every fear, every pain, every defeat has its own tear, and I bear this all before a God I have no relationship with.

I'm not sure what is proper, but I maneuver to a posture worthy of the respect I feel. With my face down and my weight on my knees, I cry out to the God of Genesis and beg for His intervention in my life. I have no one around to ask if I'm doing this right, but I bow and give Him honor in the only way I can think how.

My nose nearly scrubs the surface of the ceramic floor as I try and get as low as I possibly can. I know I have no glorious gift to offer Him and that I'm not worthy to plead my requests before Him, but if He will just allow me an opportunity to board this great boat of His, we can sail away together to a land dry and sober and full of love and life and sacrifice.

"I'll surrender. I'll surrender," I cry.

Tears crowd my eyes and mucus drips from my nose as I proclaim what my soul desires. My lips quiver, and I'm serious in my pleas. I wait only a second before I beg more from Him. I ask for an understanding of what it is I'm reading.

"I need to know all You command of me and every bit of wisdom Your Word offers. God, I have no room for mistakes. I can't do this without You."

I'm emphatic and just as quickly as I knew the answer to the question of the legitimacy of the Bible, a peace fills my spirit and it's astonishing. In a split second I no longer feel the need to cry but actually to read and get busy in a hurry with it.

I don't move, though. I'm awestruck. I think His answer is yes, He will help me. Yes, I'm sure of it. He hears me! In my excitement, I shout again, "You heard me!" and as quickly as I say this I feel silly.

"Of course He heard you, Casey," I say aloud to myself. "He is God."

I slay the hope of becoming one of His quickest scholars and shake my head as I humbly accept a more suitable role in Bible 101. I plan to read every word, cover to cover, just as it was suggested, before I leave this apartment. I lift my head from the floor and sit back against the wall behind me.

I wipe my sloppy face, and think that it's too bad with all the miracles God is doing that He does not choose to remove this burden of withdrawal from me. I almost ask but again catch myself with a very elementary response to a common consequence of sin. I guess I can rule out great and mighty conqueror of the Lord's. It's evident that I'm still a coward.

Both my head and heart pound rapidly. Fresh excitement now dwells where my ambition has long been absent, and this is the energy I use to move forward and open up the Bible. I begin again but not without reminding God that He can't afford to leave His place by my side until we are completely done reading.

I hear my silent but demanding tone, and I recant immediately, even though otherwise my comprehension might be only surface deep. I see that I need to lean on my first lessons of faith a little better than what I'm doing now if I plan to get anywhere with an invisible God.

I grasp my fresh belief and dive in to the next book, Exodus. Never have I seen more of a reason to fear someone than is evident in what I read here. God does not play around when He is ready to pour out His wrath over disobedience. There has got to be a stronger word than relief to describe my appreciation for His patience in choosing not to destroy me. I periodically stop and search for the right word to say to Him, but I have yet to give God anything better than, "Thank You. Thank You, merciful Lord."

For the first time in a long while, I'm truly honest about my condition and needs. There is nothing glamorous about where I am, but in this moment I feel richer and part of something purer than I've ever felt in all my life. The peace and safety alone tempt me to prolong my stay, but I can't contend with my newborn desire to live.

I read, read, and read some more. Nights fall and days rise. In between is a mess of every sort. My pain is deep, and my stomach is upset. My body begs for nutrition and rest, but I don't yield until I'm done. I do this only with the supernatural ability of God. To know His divine holiness sits with me in this abandoned room designed for waste impresses me to no end and encourages me to give all I have until I'm fully sober and ready to reenter the world and offer even more.

I already look on with apprehension. These four walls hold no temptation compared to the lure the free world provides naturally. I can say I love Him now and mean it, but when a challenge presents itself with difficulty, it's then that my new faith will contend with real fire and its weight be measured appropriately. At this point, I don't want to fail. The thought of my Lord witnessing me in unbridled sin sickens me, and my hatred for this lawless way springs forth.

After seven days and six nights, I come to the final book of Revelation. It proves one of the harder books to interpret and even though "blessed is the man who reads these words," I'm just glad my team wins in the end.

I think I could study the subject for years and still come up with questions about John's descriptions, times, and locations in his visions. I can see why there are many opinions on the subject. From what I learn there is only one truth, though. The many is found only in the application.

Thinking of application, I recognize that as my symptoms increase, my desire to learn the result of what I'm reading pursues me. I never understood the appeal of remembering quotes or proverbs over the years, but now I understand why reciting verses is crucial. It will remind me from whose strength I derive the ability to stay sober, and how.

As I read the final pages, my journey of more than a thousand years comes to an end, and I realize it's only the beginning. I'm reborn in my Savior and Lord Jesus Christ; I'm a new creature. I set the Bible between my legs and can't believe I've finished reading.

I look up and around past the few inches in front of me that I've been isolated to during the entire week, and my head criticizes me sharply for it. I smell myself and for a new creature, I stink horribly. I have not showered all week, and I can't blame foreign soil or overworked Marines for my poor hygiene.

With the weight of the world lifted, I try and get up from the floor. It's not easy when you've been physically lazy for a week-long venture. My flesh proves its resilience is nothing like my spiritual man, and I have to use not only the wall but sink, too, in order to steady my shifting weight.

I'm much weaker than I hoped to be. My soul, though extremely inflated, can't lift me on its own, and it reminds me that I haven't eaten in a week. My skin clings to my bones worse now than it ever has, and my outside appearance is a fiercely poor representation of what is actually going on inside of me. I'll have to work on correcting this inappropriate portrayal, being that it's so far from the truth. My soul is happy, and I feel alive. In looking at myself in the mirror, though, I can't tell.

Gray rings shadow my already silvery eyes, and the combination of the two insist that I'm a member of the walking dead. The stains on my shirt are from more than one bodily fluid, and tears and sweat are the least nasty of the few. I'm dirty, without a doubt, and it's time for me to use the bathroom for more than just a soul cleansing. I wish to rinse the week-long filth from me, and I can't wait.

I don't think I have ever been so eager to shower in all my life, and as soon as I think this, I retract the thought, remembering Iraq. I ask myself how it is that I can forget 45 days thick? I can't believe it didn't cross my mind until now, or that I didn't at least try to compare the two degrees of nasty.

I learn another new lesson. It's easy to forget my past when my present is so intense. I mentally begin making permanent notes of everything I see and feel in hopes that this moment never leaves me. I can't afford to travel this road again, and the thought of going back to the beginning terrifies me.

I would swear that I'll never wander down the same path again, but I easily recall Peter's betrayal and his promise to never fall away, even unto death. I anticipated reading the outcome, but when I did I realized that if this man, who literally followed right by Christ's side, could not just slip once but cower three times, I better not think for a second that I have a handle on this thing at all. I smile and search my bag for a change of clothing. His story did not end there, and neither does mine.

I stumble across soap and shampoo and hope the advertising on the bottle is not just a ploy. I head back to the bathroom and have the shower running in no time at all. I could use the revitalizing lift the soap and shampoo promise. The water quickly warms, and I step in. Immediately, I feel the shedding of a few pounds of gross. The bad dissolves quickly, and the rest I force away only after a solid minute of allowing running water to saturate my face.

"Thank you, God," I say as I spit out the water that runs

into my mouth. My shower feels amazing, and it's exciting to see what the day holds. I'm grateful that I'll leave different than when I entered this place. It's incredible.

I'm sober, alive, and with another chance to do things right. I turn the water off and step out of the shower that indeed proved refreshing. I can't be naive. This is not going to be easy. Just as simple as it is to wash away my filth, it can return.

I dress and make plans for what it is I'll do to avoid a relapse. I have to find a church. I have to face Jayden. I have to get a job. I have to prepare for Steven, and just as I plan another very large goal in a short amount of time, my stomach growls. I have to eat! Nourishment reminds me that slowing down and taking one issue at a time might be a wise idea. Things have priorities, and I need to get mine in order.

I look in the mirror one last time. I didn't pack a razor, and my five o'clock shadow times seven days breeds a beard that explains things well. I comb through it as best as my fingers will allow. I retrieve my new favorite tool and gladly turn the light off behind me. I collect all that I bring with me and see the foolishness I entered the apartment with.

I was so mad that I would have easily killed this stranger in my anger, but who knew that he would turn out to be my hero? Again, I smile at the unseen protection I have had throughout all of this. I can't make up a story this unbelievably good. I wonder, if I share it in detail will others think it's a lie?

My smile fades. I'm sure to look in the face of disbelief often. It's only fair according to my behavior that I accept these unwilling faces; however, I can easily see that it may crush me. While I know my heart, others can't see that I tell the truth, and my track record since being here proves only that I'm unworthy of any substantial amount of trust.

I see the need to plan my approach in advance. I figure in doing so I might avoid an overreaction on my part. If I, even for a short time, allow my desires to exceed the fine balance of grace and patience God extends to me, I may make matters worse than they already are. Then I'll face a whole new set of problems.

A story of a change in ways is easier believed when there is supporting evidence. I have nothing but words, and mine no longer persuade those who know me. I can swear on the Bible and offer to pledge my sincerity in blood, but in something so radical, I fear the brand as "a desperate man" might just end up being as detrimental as my addiction itself.

It's going to be a real challenge when I'm forced to contend against my own history. I pray the Lord speaks for me. I take a few final glances around the room, and I see I have no right to demand respect from anyone. While I want to pick up where I left off, it's not my right but a privilege.

I slide my bag up my arm and over my shoulder. I'm responsible for what I've read and what has happened in this room. I can't walk out of here and claim ignorance one day. Chills run across my arms. There is nothing ordinary about any of this. God is real. I know it, and He knows I know it.

I turn and leave the past where it is. I walk down the familiar hall a final time and plan never to return to a time so dark and callous. As I move towards a new life, I gain momentum in each step. My energy has not returned, but I'm driven by possibility. I'm a new man with a new life, and I wonder what this new world is going to look like.

I fumble into the elevator. Even though I'm sober, I still feel a little off. My legs are sluggish and don't maintain my balance as well as they usually do. I hope this odd sensation improves after I eat. I'm unsure what this stems from, but my lack of confidence in my own stability causes me to grab the railing at my waist. I look around and pick a spot to stick with. I ride for only three floors, but it's enough to throw me off kilter.

I rejoice in the option of exiting the elevator and leap forward with enthusiasm undeserved by the wet floor I nearly slip and fall on. I steady myself and realize that I need something solid in more ways than just food. I turn and aim towards the light of day. I squint the closer I get to natural light, having only been exposed to a dimly lit apartment for a week. The rays from the sun seem extreme, and even though I haven't made it outside yet, I already regret my failure in packing sunglasses.

I pass the doorman I was beginning to think I had dreamed up. I wave a final farewell, and he responds automatically, smiling through a mound of wrinkles. I doubt he remembers who I am, but it's not important. I hope to never see him again. I'm not ill-mannered, but I'm almost free from my attachment to this place; while what transpired here is amazing, I don't want to ever repeat it.

I reach the door that will open a new chapter in my life. I hesitate—so much is required of me. I don't look forward to revealing my darkest hours to those I love, but in this honest and humble tale lies my salvation, and that I'll never regret sharing.

As a matter of fact, I'm eager to expose the victory I obtain in Christ even to strangers, like the waitress Sarah, whose motto I only now understand. My nerves pick up their pace, and my gut reaction is to move. I need to start in a positive direction, and being that I'm literally starving, the coffee café is a perfect idea.

I step outside, and a gust of wind welcomes me back to the land of the living. I allow myself a second to adjust, and while I wait my senses flare in ways I haven't experienced in a long time. The dullness of my former life is lifting, and I can better distinguish between the sounds I hear, the things

I smell, and the pains I feel.

The most intense sensation of all is the emptiness of my barren stomach and the weakness that results. I carry back with me only what is mine, but with no energy reserve to draw from, the longer I travel the heavier this burden is. I almost need to call out and ask for strength to sustain me. I know I won't get very far if God refuses. I'm eager to see Him pull me through.

I walk the streets that once aggravated me and see no need to harbor resentment towards them. They are permanent, and I see now it was only me who was flighty. As I make my way to the parking deck, I hope my truck is safe and unscathed by my long-time absence. Relief sweeps over me as soon as I see my beloved truck, and it's perfect timing. I'm ready to lighten my load. As soon as I'm in range, I speed up my walk.

My doors unlock the moment it recognizes the electronic signal I send, and I don't hesitate in climbing in behind the wheel. I'm re-learning many things about myself that I have chosen to overlook. I'm sorely out of shape enough to the point of embarrassment. I must improve my fitness.

My to-do's are growing rapidly, and I have not even made it home yet. If I keep this pace, I fear it may develop into something too large to tackle. I settle my creeping anxiety and remind myself to take one issue at a time. I sit for a second and catch the breath I too easily expel. I gather my overly anxious thoughts and feel pressed to check in with Jayden. It's unfair to allow his worry to persist as long as it has.

I reach for my duffel bag, hopefully for the last time. When collecting my things, I didn't stop to check if my phone is actually broken or just disassembled. I shuffle the items around until I collect all four pieces that make my phone complete. I attach them together the way they are designed and hold down the power button to reveal its fate.

While waiting for the manufacturer's icon to appear, I almost hope it doesn't work. I can see where keeping connections could be tempting, and I do not need extra help in sinning. I shun the idea of another encouraging me along, even unintentionally.

My answer appears. I face my first temptation despite my desire for it never to exist. My phone works. Before I decide what I should do, it begins alerting me of week-long missed calls and messages. My choice is now tougher than a moment ago.

I click on the envelope and compose a quick text to Jayden: "Coming home today."

As soon as I'm sure of its delivery, I unroll my window and chuck the phone over the side of the deck. I hear its sure defeat and in the crash, I can't believe I just did that. God must really be helping me along, because that was a $600 phone I just destroyed.

I start my engine to drown out my complaints, and in hearing the roar of 400 horsepower, I'm encouraged by how fast I can get to the coffee house if I step on it. I pull out and round the outside corner. The sun blinds me. To my relief my sunglasses are in my console, and I seek their immediate aid in blocking out the intrusive rays.

It's chilly outside, but I keep the window half down in order to take in the fresh stink of New York City. It took a little getting used to when I first moved here, but now the smell reminds me that I'm still alive and indeed not alone.

Fresh peanuts tell me I'm heading in the right direction, and in less time than I'm used to I see my destination. The coffee café looks busy, but I'm still interested. I find parking a couple of blocks over and don't mind in the least the extra effort it takes to get there.

Walking the right path is inspiring. While I don't have

much to brag about yet, I increase in joy. I'm heading towards the cross instead of away from it, and this fact alone gives me peace. Simplifying my life may not be effortless, but I do see how the Lord's yoke is easier and the burden of circumstance much lighter with Him guiding my way. What I used to look at and see negatively is now a view with great possibility.

I smile while I step around the feet of a homeless man I cross in my trail leading to Sarah's place. Unlike the last couple hundred times before, I don't get far without something reminding me emphatically that I still carry a large amount of cash in my pocket. I continue my pace only to find myself U-turn and retrace my steps back to the man I passed. I reach him, open my wallet, and relinquish a $100 bill. He looks up at me in what seems to be utter amazement, and I give him a couple more $100 bills.

"Jesus must really love you," I say and walk away feeling the same odd way I did when I chucked my phone out the window.

I can't believe I just did that. I wonder how much my new life choice is going to cost me in the end. I realize my freedoms in posing the question.

I change my pattern and ask silently if this growing compulsion is something I should get used to. It takes only a few seconds before I again suppose I already know the answer. If I don't quench it, it will probably grow to a deafening roar. I wonder how far I would have gotten if my answer had been no. I realize I don't want to know the answer to that.

I keep moving and practically leap through the doorway that offers breakfast on the other side. The smell of things edible hits me abruptly, and as a result my stomach cries out. My mouth salivates, and I swallow so that it's not obvious to those around me. A young woman approaches me and offers a seat that is quite possibly the very same booth

I sat in a week ago.

I slide in and adjust to the slick vinyl cushion offered to me. She places a menu on the table, and I watch as she is off to greet more new arrivals before I even register she has left. If my wit was quicker, I could have saved her the effort in leaving the menu behind. I already know what I want, but now I'll be forced to look at the alluring images of grossly attractive foods. I have only felt this way once in my past, and I recall my need then to never focus on what I do not have.

Our resupply convoy being destroyed by an IED was not as bad as it could've been. But when we all began to feel the pangs of hunger, I would have argued it was. I remember daydreaming of steak and potatoes in the first few days of hunger, and before I knew it I made myself sick with desire.

My first bite into the thigh of a butchered goat tasted nothing like the meal of my mind, but it did cure me from minor starvation. What I learned is not to tease myself. If I can't have it, I shouldn't think about it. It worked then, and I hope it will work now, at least until my food arrives and my need for sustenance is again fulfilled.

I push the menu to the far end of the table and wait only a second more before being greeted again.

"Sir?" the waitress says.

Teenage help is typical in coffee shops, but this girl hardly looks of legal age. Instead of wasting her time, I look behind her for my more preferred waitress, Sarah.

She interrupts my search with a monotone, "Good morning and welcome to Dan's Coffee and Danish Café. How may I take your order?"

What I hear surprises me, and I ask her to repeat the name. "Whose Coffee and Danish Café?" I ask but only half-listen as my attention focuses on a broader look around me.

"Dan's Coffee and Danish Café." She repeats the well-rehearsed verse a little more maturely this time, but it's not impressive due to my state of confusion. Attached to the walls of the café are notes written to Dan, whom I'm confident is the owner.

I'm not close enough to read their contents, but I recognize the abbreviations that follow the body of words. They are all signed by those with rank. Their initials reveal their authority, and I absolutely do not understand what I'm seeing. I can feel my brow form the letter V, and my clueless reaction signals my waitress.

"Excuse me, sir. Are you alright? Do you need help?" The childlike voice returns but is genuine in its nurturing nature.

I can't imagine the look on my face that causes her to react this way. I do indeed need help but not the kind this young girl can offer.

"Ugh…" I mumble. "Is Sarah working today? I would really like her to wait on me, if possible. I need to thank her for her wonderful services the other day."

My mumble turns cheery right at the end, but it does not draw a smile from her lips. The poor girl now has her own unique crinkle stamped across her face, and it's without a doubt for a different reason than mine.

"Who?" This time she asks me to repeat myself, and in my response I elaborate in order to help her along.

"Sarah. I would like Sarah to serve me, if possible. You know, the waitress who has a very kind smile and walks with a slight limp. I think she works this shift, if I'm not mistaken. She was here when I came in last week and helped me in more ways than one."

"Sorry, mister." Her response is immediately discouraging. "I have worked here my whole summer break, and I don't know of any Sarah at all. You must be confused with the cupcake shop down the street. They serve all the same things we do. You should try there."

As I listen to what she is saying, I shift to a state of pure flux. I'm not sure what is happening. I know I'm not crazy, and I know that I'm in the right place. I met Sarah here, and she slipped over that rug with the small tear only 20 feet or so from where I sit now. It's still visibly a hazard and in this my sanity relaxes its scary accusation that I'm losing the last bit of wit I carry.

I hold my tongue from responding to her matter-of-factness, simply because I don't know what to expect next. The young waitress must be growing annoyed by my indecisive behavior, because her next question proves it so. It's demanding and without concern for my mental condition.

"Sir, did you want to place an order, then, or are you going to try the shop down the street?"

While I'm uncertain of the chaos in my brain, I'm confident in my need to feed myself. "I'll take the House Special with a tall drip coffee and small orange juice, please."

She jots my order on her fiercely used pad, collects the unwanted menu, and walks away, surely finding relief from another slightly less deranged customer.

I must appear the way I'm feeling. This is all very strange, and I'm having a hard time computing the facts at this point in my journey. As soon as she leaves, I stand and move to get a closer look at the letters that are distracting me. The first I come to is hand-written in ultra-tiny uppercase on what seems to be an ordinary piece of notebook paper.

Dan,

I found the Bible you left just in the nick of time. I owe you my life. I was planning to kill myself the evening you came knocking, and had it been under any other circumstance, I would have never opened the door. I hope the girl is okay. I passed the Word on to another and hope Its effects are the same for them as they are for me.

PFC

I re-read the letter and am blown away. I open my mouth wide, and my teeth are hidden behind my hands, which cup them as a result of pure shock. If this letter is legit, I'm not the only one to receive the Bible. I think about the odds of me walking into this place and question what is really happening here. Could it be that there is more to my story?

I move on to the next piece of paper; it's concealed behind an old, roped brass frame. I'm so eager to discover its origin I nearly bump into the booth it's posted by. I do not look to see if it's occupied. My only care this second is to know what the paragraph reveals. My answer is written in smeared black ink. In its damaged state, I have to concentrate on every letter in order to read it in full.

Dan,

I was going to kill you when you took off and left me out in the desert with only a book and backpack of rations. I could not believe you were so arrogant to approach me with something as simple and crazy as just reading its pages. I intended to destroy you right after I wiped out my wife and her new lover, but ... I'm glad you left me. You forced me to consider living life another way. I would have died in prison had you not the courage to stand against my rage, and for that I owe you my life. Call it "an exchange for freedom." As long as I live, brother, I'm in your debt!

Thank you,

3SG

P.S. Nice touch in sending someone to pick me back up. Glad she found me.

This is amazing. It's no fluke that I landed in possession of the traveling Bible. Someone intentionally gave me the book to help me change my life, but who knows this story and how it works? I rack my brain and believe no one close to me could be responsible. Jayden doesn't keep secrets from me very well, and Jacob neither lives around here nor knows enough people in the area to pull off such a complicated conspiracy.

It's a difficult task to pique the interest of a junkie, and not only that but to keep it long enough to allow time for change to occur. I breathe deeply and shake my head from side to side. I disagree that it's someone close to me, but it seems these two letters are quite personal.

I need to see the written collection in its entirety. If I hurry, I should have time to investigate a couple more letters before my meal arrives. I move along, pressing tightly against the wall where possible until I come across the next letter. I can see this one is going to be just as intriguing as the two preceding it.

To Dan, if that's even your real name,

Sandy's death nearly killed me and when they finally pronounced my only son permanently brain dead, too, I couldn't handle it. Sandy and John were my life, and without them I couldn't breathe. I gave everything I had to my wife and child, and when they passed, so did I. I was empty and alone and without hope inside of me.

The extent of the accident reached much further than just my own suffering. Another family with a child was out there fighting for their lives. Knowing this and that I had quit but was responsible, tortured me beyond anything ever could. Death seemed reasonable.

I want you to know that the Bible you put on the edge of my chair at the end of the funeral changed my life. It was the only thing I hadn't tried to ease the pain in my life. When I took it home and forced myself to read it, I cried. God understands what it's like to lose a son.

I imagined Him cold, hard, distant, and absolutely vacant from my life. Instead, I found him loving, full of mercy, consistent, and sovereign. He turned out to be the one

thing that helped me get up from where I gave up.
I just wanted to say thank you to whoever you are for what
you stand for. I realize we may never meet, but I want you
to know that I passed the Bible on in the same manner of
hope it was given to me, and the kid who got it really
needs it. I pray he also finds his way.
Faithfully yours,
LCP

The waitress whistles for my attention, and my acknowl-
edgement does not reflect my true enthusiasm. I'm starving,
but these words are deep and can't be walked away from
lightly. This is serious. People, namely men of uniform, are
out there helping each other in a very different level of war-
fare, and what is happening as a result of their efforts is
amazing.

I walk over to the young girl and greet her a second time.
I tell her of my appreciation for the quick preparation of my
food, and for this I get my first genuine grin. She nods in
agreement and the words, "My pleasure" flow out of her
mouth without any extra effort at all. She leaves after making sure I need nothing else, and I can't wait to be alone.

The steam draws my attention, and I start in as soon as
her back is turned. I'm halfway finished before I even realize I never said the blessing. I easily neglect my duties as a
Christian and hope God can overlook my human condition.

The food tastes amazing, and I have much to be thankful
for. I don't know why I was chosen to be reached out to, but
for whatever signal I sent up, I'm glad the blessings came
down. If I never have another thing in life, I'm full in this
moment. I'm completely undeserving of such great efforts,
but God sent others to sacrifice their time and reach out to
me anyway.

I acknowledge this and feel a tear form in the corner of
my eye. I quickly tilt my head back to swallow it down. I

have never been one to cry much and this twice in one week thing—one of those while in public—isn't going to accommodate my male ego very well at all. I secretly hope this is a passing part of the packaged deal. I can't imagine walking around as a constant ball of swirling emotions.

After I'm sure that it won't fall, and I'm safe from being found out, I look back down at the casual china in front of me. My meal has fast disappeared, and my overly stuffed belly aches its shame. My aggression is filling my gut so rapidly it stretches my stomach prematurely, and a pain in my side reeks of an onset of up-and-coming indigestion. I force a burp in the politest way possible and cover my mouth to excuse myself. My meal was delicious, but I'm not satisfied. There is far more to digest hanging on the walls around me and not enough time to do all I desire.

I would pick up and resume where I left off reading before my meal came, but experience tells me that jumping up too soon might have consequences. I decide to use my minutes wisely and force myself to wait 10 before I resume.

In doing so, I allow my mind room to roam. I run my hands over my unaccustomed stubble and backtrack through the memories of the different events I've collected. I rewind far enough, and the moment I first receive the Bible comes into view.

I remember being very desperate and extremely vulnerable, but the order in which these two occur is confusing. What stands out most is that the entire incident is broken and in more pieces than I would hope for in trying to solve a puzzle. No fact is definite, and the tiny segments in which they are revealed offer more likely just parts to a much bigger picture.

I vaguely see myself signing something and getting high, but much past that everything is bleak. Even worse was waking up in the absence of certainty, substance, and solid subject matter and an old book lending itself as my only clue to what happened to me. I see clearly the dilemma of inhibition, and it reinforces my choice to no longer participate in mind-altering drugs. I can't determine how much of my life is not just jumbled but lost all together as a result of my dependency.

I can barely keep the last week straight in my mind, and I lived it sober. I can't imagine the moments I forfeited to intoxication, and again I think of a question I do not want to know the answer to. If this is proof of a typical day in addiction, I can expect many changes now that I'm fully awake and aware.

Skipping forward, I believe in miracles, but what is happening is surreal. I don't know how I can successfully tell this story without it sounding like an embellishment. It really is unbelievable in many ways, and I'm likely to tell of it and be scorned, whether it be for stupidity or just plain naivety in general. Jayden may hear and even develop a new concern for my mental health that has nothing to do with chemicals at all.

I sigh loudly. I want to tell him my story and have him not only believe me but support me. If I begin and he is not ready, I have to be sensitive no matter if I'm good at it or not. I embrace a hard subject, and my emotional instability concerning it. I know I have to trust the Lord in His timing for restoration.

I learned of His promises just this week and know that what is spoken by Him cannot be voided. I preach to myself that I should know better, but I'm still scared of Jayden's rejection. My current hopes and dreams involve a complete healing in our friendship, and if there isn't, it will be a weight of heavy sorrow.

I sit only a few more seconds before I collect my energy and stand. I shake my doubts with ill regard and choose not to focus on what has yet to happen. I don't want to lose my hope or my table, so I ask my waitress for a refill of coffee and the check only when she has a free moment. She agrees, and I'm pleased to wander the café while I wait.

I don't intend to leave this place until I review every story, but the letters are so intense it may be harder than I think. I hesitate in my next step, but it lasts only a second until it passes. I need to find out how this whole thing operates, and these letters, while difficult, are a tool to assist in my understanding.

I walk up to the next letter and before reading, I pause again. I have never considered an operation that saves not only the bodies of men but their spirits, too. It's a noble idea, and I can't imagine the story behind Dan himself. Whatever compelled and led him to begin such a dynamic task has to be a tale all its own, and I would love to know its entirety. I chuckle aloud to myself. A week ago, I would not believe my own ears. If I had heard his story back then, I would not be only skeptical but condescending, too.

The next letter dangles on the outstretched arm of a rusty nail. Its overlapping sides require me to unfold the dirty cloth in order to see what it says. It's written on what looks to be the sleeve of an old, burnt t-shirt, but I could be mistaken. This one is sure to be interesting, and I gain intrigue before I even know the details. Right away, it's surprising. It's written in the form of a poem, and I don't expect this method of storytelling.

For the wall, I'll call you Dan, but I know that's not your name.
You left this book by my burning house, and I thought it was a game.
I wandered the streets alone and without, nearly starving to death.
I found a lonely soul to share with, and he simply offered me meth.

I took what I took and gave what I gave and at the end of every day,
I couldn't see in the place I made and prayed for a lighted way.
At the moment of sorrow, in my final despair, I remembered I still carried you,
And decided to read without any lead, and it led me to a pew.
Now, here I sit to this very day, helping to save our few.
It's never too late, at any given rate, and I learned this all through you.
GySgt

Again, my mouth plops open, and my mind freezes in its former doubt. This is what awe must feel like, because I can't explain the compelling need for me to fall flat on my face and worship. I can't believe I get to be a part of something so great. My pride swells, and I realize what I have failed to consider until now.

I, too, have the privilege of thanking Dan, and not only that, but possess the specific instrument that inspires all of these people to change. I have a new responsibility. I'll be sad to relinquish my title as owner, but I'm no longer entitled at this point. It's my turn to seek out and nurture an environment and opportunity to help another overcome.

I look around for a pen but don't see one. People are nearby, and I should just ask if they have one, but I have always been uncomfortable in borrowing. My lifelong shyness is still the nuisance it always has been. I consider running back to my truck, but it's a silly idea. I need to be able to face discomfort if I expect to participate in something so grand.

I clear my throat and proceed to interrupt the breakfast of a business woman with a very large purse. As I do, I remember my check. A pen will be waiting with it, and my nerves and anxiety will prove completely unnecessary.

"I'm sorry, ma'am." I blush as I bring my hand back from calling for her attention.

I can feel the temperature in my face spike, and I jet back to my booth as fast as I can before I accidentally see the reason I don't speak much to strangers. I collapse in the cushion as soon as I return and appreciate the pen waiting alongside a full account of my order.

I pull my wallet, along with everything else from my back pocket, and tuck the appropriate payment neatly into the corner fold. I sort through the pile until I find what I'm looking for. I borrow the pen from under the clip, and separate the adhesive from the joints of my bank's withdrawal envelope.

I plan to use it as a backdrop on which I'll compose my letter to Dan, but as I begin writing I don't know where to start. I accept that this is going to take more than a few minutes, and when my waitress comes back I explain that I plan to sit for awhile longer but for her not to worry.

"I'm going to need the table for another half hour or so, miss," I explain, "but I promise I'll tip generously in order to cover your troubles. If you don't mind, would you bring me two blueberry muffins to go? This should make everyone happy."

My young waitress shows every one of her freshly permanent teeth in response to my extra efforts in accommodating her inconvenience.

She is enthusiastic and responds by claiming, "No extra trouble at all, sir. Stay as long as you need."

Her grin is most certainly one of joy, and she hurries away, looking rather pleased by the news of a larger tip. I smile at how easy it is to appease her and hope my letter will carry with it the same manner of speed and excitement.

I look at the odd shape of the paper I chose and invoke

the seriousness I need in order to begin. Once I can sound the chords of my deepest thinking, I press my pen to the paper and commence in writing what is difficult for me to put into words. It takes me almost an hour to complete, but when my task is done I feel a sense of accomplishment and, to my surprise, an equality again with those who serve.

I pay what I promised and leave after I hang my letter on the wall with the others. I walk away, not with a thousand details but rather with simple instructions on how to help a brother in need. My guide is an old book, and being that it doesn't audibly respond when I ask it something, I hope I interpret correctly what love is. This job will not succeed without it.

I return to my truck with more than I left. I have an assignment, and the pleasure of serving is again mine. While it will not look as it did when I was overseas, it's nonetheless important and just as necessary. Many brothers are out here without hope, being overwhelmed by the circumstances of life, and it doesn't have to be this way. I'm not exactly sure where I'll start first, but my ideas are plenty and my needs slight.

Exhilaration envelops my still aching body. I hop in my truck with this burst of energy and check my mental to-do list again. What I can't overlook is my appeal to Jayden. I'll need his help in order to pull this off, but hard hearts hinder not help. I hope I haven't waited too long.

I buckle up and start my engine. Although the belt is restraining, I'm free to move. I extend my arms out as far as they can reach in order to stretch all possibility. I skim the lining on the roof of my cab on the way down, and the fact that I notice this small sensation surprises me. I relax a little more, but I still can't seem to suck in enough cool air to slow the rising temperature of my heart.

Just thinking about what comes next shatters my level of

confidence. I have to go home, and it will not be easy. More has been added to my already unbelievable story, and I haven't the slightest clue how he will respond. Jayden is awesome, but people have their limits.

I turn my truck around and face the direction of home. I pull out and what I approach is a field full of influence, and the consequence of passing through it is an altered life. I drive forward into what will be the greatest venture of my time here on Earth, and I pray with all I have in me that I get it right.

My personal margins are without limit, and my goal is to impact the life of another. I'm not sure that I'm ready, but I don't see much of a choice. The door is open, and it's time to pass through.

Tiny bumps cause the hair on my arms to stand on end, and my knees do not find the rest they were expecting. I tremble while driving, but I don't know how to stop something I've never quite suffered in this way.

I have fought many battles of war. In all my experience, I only shake like I'm doing now when it's a life or death situation. If I don't pay attention to this detail, I'm a fool. My response to this invisible conflict spells the seriousness of what is before me.

I don't know if it has to do with the fact that I feel totally unworthy, or that in my sober mind I understand what my challenge is, but either way I pray God never departs from me. I can see I'm far from strong enough to succeed in this mission alone.

In acknowledging this, my knees cease their springy dance. I appreciate the break, and I'm only a block away from home. I want to slow down, but it's the one day since I moved here that there is no need. No one is directly in front of me or behind me to justify a speed change at all, and it's strange. My pace is steady; it's surely the Lord's doing.

If it were up to me, I would have accidentally forgotten something at the café and turned around to retrieve it. I would not completely back out, just give myself more time to practice my skills in communicating. If I keep honest in the course I'm on, I should just admit, I'm scared to death.

The time it must have taken for someone to carry out the large goal of reaching me inspires me to keep planning as I go. I vaguely remember Scripture declaring that a noble man plans noble things and on those he stands. I need to proceed methodically and full of purpose if I'm going to be effective for Christ and win back the trust of my brother's heart.

I review the elaborate lengths some unknown stranger went for me, and I try to find my guts. I know there is purpose in all that has transpired and even more in what is to come. I just have to be willing to face the issues that will teach me. When I see Jayden, it will be a lesson, and growing is painful.

What I can't foresee is in the hands of the Lord, regardless of my anxiety over it. I know this, but it isn't easy to relinquish these feelings. The temptation to flee is strong, and I intentionally have to turn from it with every second that closes in on my next task. Jayden is closer now, and I can feel the squeeze of shame press against me. It's time for me to confess and ask for the forgiveness I would never admit I need.

I return to the tear that swelled over my friend's eye. While the Lord knows I would like to expel the memories of hurt from my life all together, he allows me to keep them for now. Maybe the impression will be enough to force me to never again comply with the likes of Satan. Perhaps the imprint will keep me humble and remind me that I'm a dependent creature.

What I've done can't be undone, only made right over a

period of time. I must bear the resemblance of change, and in this transparent state shine the light given to me. I can show Jayden better that I can tell him, anyway. I have never communicated well, and Jayden knows this. I continue driving and am only seconds away now. In seeing our building come into view, my pleas for help turn audible.

"Please, God, give me the words I can't find." My voice cracks and I hope this is not a preview of what is to come. I don't want to sound like someone who is not confident of his change.

I find my own personal parking spot, which has been vacant for a solid week now. As I pull in, I look for the last time through the glass that separates me from the cold world outside. My life will change within the next few minutes, whether I'm prepared or not.

With this in mind, I jump out and leave everything but my bag and Bible behind. It's chilly but soon I'll be in the middle of a heated conversation and no additional clothing will be needed.

I march to my apartment, but not with confidence. I'm shaky and my demeanor is unsure. I lower my head in order that I not fumble, and I meet my destination quicker than I like. My apartment door is becoming a regular obstacle. I stare at it like any participant would and can barely force my hand to turn the knob that challenges me.

I finally do and step over the welcome mat, my head glued to the floor for security. Who knew honesty would be so tough. I easily lower the baggage I carry, and pride can be found nowhere within me. I set down the heavy weight, and as I do I notice that I'm not alone. I don't have to look further to know who owns the boots I stare at. It is Jayden. He stands only feet in front of me, and whether I'm ready or not my first new trial begins.

I slowly follow the boots up and concentrate on the presence of their owner. Without intention or warning, I don't make it past his waist. I crumble to the ground beneath me, and my knees hit the floor hard. I close my eyes and try to temporarily escape the scene I've caused. There is no absconding. I lift my hands in tight fists in order to beat my way from this situation, but they strike nothing but my own face as the tears from my soul escape uncontrollably down my cheeks.

I can't make myself talk; I try but nothing comes out that is understandable. Unruly sobbing is not the method I envisioned using to explain myself, but it's the only thing that comes out even close to right. I'm broken for the pain I have caused my brother, and in searching for a way to express myself, I weep. I fight to breathe in confidence between the gaps of tears, but I'm unsuccessful. I finally just extend my arms out to God for help.

Amazingly, I feel His answer, and a warm touch causes me to open my eyes abruptly. Jayden is reaching underneath my arms and literally picking me up off the ground.

Once stable, these same arms surround me and offer me the forgiveness I do not deserve. His embrace is that of God's, unconditional and undeserved. Brotherhood is for a lifetime, and in seeing the behavior I neglect to perform myself, I'm grateful for the mercy God continually extends to me. It's another reason to again stoop to a position of humility, but my brother's grip is firm, and I don't believe he will ever let me fall again. For at least a solid minute, my brother welcomes me home.

In pulling away, I see that I'm not the only one with a wet face. Tears fall from Jayden's eyes but for a different reason than the last time. Joy is beautiful to see, especially when it involves the birth of something new. Here and now is a fresh start. I acknowledge this and can't believe I almost forfeited the reunion on behalf of being yellow.

It's amazing how much the world whispers discouragement in my ear. If I would have given in, who knows what kind of feelings a later date could have brought about? I thank God in my heart and smile in response to Jayden's reaction.

My condition must truly be self-explanatory because immediately, without conversation, he ushers me into the kitchen to give me something to eat. I know I must look extra pitiful because what he is choosing is nothing but fruits, vegetables, powders, and the weird seed things he always insists I add to my diet for health reasons. I hope what I call his "seed things" don't make me sick. I know his hopes are to rejuvenate me, but my stomach is still somewhat weak.

I allow his attempt to repair me, and I sit quietly while the machine finely shreds into the conglomeration he chooses. Once blending is complete, he sits down beside me with an equal glass of his own. I take a shallow sip, and he nearly finishes his in two large gulps. As soon as he returns the cup to the table the words "Tell me about it" come out of his mouth.

I smile again and in assessing the depth of his true sincerity, I see a complete genuineness. His eyes are eager, and this is all I need to begin the tale that transformed my life. I start off with the fact that I once would never declare, and Jayden is not surprised. He sits with an open mind and an open heart, and this is all I can ask for.

The minutes turn to hours, and the hours pass the day. I take him with me to the bar, the bank, the apartment, and the diner. I do not skip a detail, and Jayden shows little discomfort. He listens to each and every twist that comes into play and questions only what happens next. Well after midnight, I express the emotional impact this entire event has had on my soul, and I finally share what is the most important fact of the entire story: my salvation.

To my surprise, Jayden has known all along who Jesus Christ is and makes an enormous confession of his own. When Jayden says that this is where he derives his notorious strength from, it makes perfectly good sense. I start to ask him why he never mentioned this sooner, but I stop myself. I didn't make talking to me easy for anyone. I feel shame and joy at the same time. God is and has always been around me from the very beginning of my journey.

Pieces on a grand scale come together much clearer now, and I can't believe I didn't recognize all of this sooner. I guess what they say about the intoxicated being blind is true. Jayden's attitude in many ways does resemble Christ. I was blessed early on and didn't even know it.

The most incredible outcome of the evening is when Jayden declares, "Aww, man, count me all in. Whatever I can do to help, just let me know. I definitely want to be a part of something like this."

To hear that he not only believes me but supports me to the degree of participating himself gives me a whole new reason to burst into tears, but I purposefully refrain. I have lost enough manhood from my ego in one day, and I don't think I can suffer another tearful trauma without passing out from sheer exhaustion.

Noticing my continual shifting, Jayden recommends we both get some shut eye, and it's a relief that I can continue in the morning. I don't argue with him, and I'm the first to obey his suggestion. When I stand, the weight I carried in with me is completely gone. While I still have no strength, I'm sure I'll move much easier now that I've handled the business that weighed me down.

I say goodnight and head to my room. I hope it's cleaner than I remember. I can only imagine the mess I left, and before I see it I make a promise to myself to clean up first thing tomorrow, no matter what.

I open my door, and to my surprise my room is neater than it has ever been. A pile of clothing lay freshly washed and folded on my neatly made bed. My trashcan is empty and washed clean. The mountain of miscellaneous items spilling out of my closet is completely gone, and all has been returned to its assigned place. I scan the room from left to right, and again I see the love that I neglected to notice. Jayden is one heck of a guy. Relief pats me on the back because he above all knows I really hate cleaning, even on a good day.

I remove my shoes and lay the neat piles of clothing on top of my dresser. I'm so tired that finding where they go can be done in the morning. I don't even pull back my comforter but slam my body into its plush welcome instead. Before I can concentrate on it, I fall asleep.

CHAPTER EIGHT

Planning for Steven to arrive is exciting, but waking up and realizing that all my efforts are a dream is not. I roll over and try to keep the images fresh, but as my feet hit the floor they are already fading.

My back is stiff, and my tongue is stuck to the roof of my mouth. I feel like I've been sleeping for days. My morning is still not what it should be, and if I try to compare it to what it used to be, I'll only grow more frustrated with how long it takes to get back to what I consider a good normal.

I keep my seat on the edge of my bed and remind myself that it has only been one day over a week. I continue to recite that it will get better tomorrow, but so far the better is closer to the same, so I try not to think about it. I'll definitely need help again from God if I'm going to make it through another day feeling like this.

I hit my knees to pray, and once down I begin to see a pattern develop. I make my needy requests known. I pick myself

up off the floor with new hope that it won't be like this forever. I head to my bedroom door wearing the same clothes I
had on yesterday, and it's surprising that the thought of maybe
changing into something a little less restraining just now
crosses my mind. I suppose drugs have done more damage
to my thinking than I give them credit for.

I stand at the door and instead of trying to make up a de-
ceitful story before I head out, I soak in the appreciation of
real freedom. I have no need to become someone else. I'm
in the beginning of a new life, and it's no secret. I relax
knowing that I faced a huge challenge yesterday and didn't
cower out even though I wanted to. I'm fast learning that
it's not necessarily the circumstance but what you do with
the circumstance--that makes the difference.

I smile as I head towards the kitchen, and again Jayden
has food prepared for me when I arrive. I bite into the loaded
omelet he left on the kitchen table and although good, it's
cold. I look at the time on the clock on the wall and see it's
just before noon. I've slept half my day away, wasting valu-
able opportunity to make preparations for Steven, who is
coming sooner rather than later.

I try and remember the plans in my dreams, and I still can't
recall it like I want to. I'm glad I made mention to Jayden last
night about Steven's coming and that he has a few ideas of
his own. I still feel a little foggy, and his clear mind will be
useful in order to get everything done that we need to.

Jayden is completely confident that we can help Steven
out, even with our limited space. We both agree that there
are things he will need, but a trip to the local department
store should strike many of these problems off of our list.
I'm most excited about how well he will do when he realizes
he is permanently welcome and that he may stay here with
us not just as long as he needs to, but wants to.

I picture Steven in our barracks. He is a big guy from

every angle. I'm not looking forward, especially with his history, to have to tell him my former approach to life like I did with Jayden. But it's only fair he knows the truth. We are not as close, but we are friends and brothers the same. He will be rightfully disappointed, regardless of how deep our connection is.

Growing up the way he did, seeing what he saw, disgust is natural even for the careless of heart. When he finds out that I chose to use drugs, he will more than likely give me the cursing Jayden should have given. Shamefully, I consider for a split second to just not tell him, but the fact that I'm a slug will say something. Better he hear it with remorse than to find out when I fall behind without purpose.

"Good afternoon, brother," Jayden says. "I'm glad you decided to join the land of the living."

His pleasant smile interrupts my thinking but makes giving me a hard time not so bad. He points to his wristwatch and hustles my breakfast along without the need to speak out loud.

"Plastic storage bins and extra bedding is our first goal, but since we have less than forty-eight hours, we need to get a move on."

"Forty-eight hours?" I question his estimation, but when he tells me that Steven emailed him this morning to tell him he changed his flight dates, I see our need to hurry ... and to be more diligent about checking my email.

"Wow, really?" I say. "I've got to get moving. That's faster than I expected. Are you sure you don't mind helping out? I don't want to take you from whatever it was you had planned to do today." I ask politely, but Jayden's frown that follows is too much.

"Casey," he says, "I work for myself developing websites. I can do it in my sleep. Now come on, go get in the shower. We've got stuff to do."

I look at my friend, and a grin sneaks out from underneath my skinny cheeks. I can't make sense of why I ever wanted to avoid help like this. My brother's goofy grimace is exactly what I need to stay accountable. I chuckle all the way to the shower.

"It's one-fifteen, good brother. You might need to work on your get up." Another hard time from Jayden that isn't so hard. He grabs our jackets and hands me mine.

"I know, I plan to. It's work just being up and moving around," I explain to Jayden. "It's a lot harder than I thought it would be. I keep telling myself it will get better, but it hasn't yet. I hope this doesn't last long. I don't have a bit of energy."

He simply replies, "Well, don't think about it then. We've got better stuff to do."

He is much more enthusiastic than me, but his response is welcome, and I need reminders that not everything is about me. We indeed have a very important task to complete, and I'm not the focus of attention.

I nod my head and obey his orders. I toss him the keys, and he isn't surprised that I relinquish my vehicle so willingly. It's obvious that I'm not up to par, and I'm grateful for the fact that he isn't pushing me. In all honesty, today does feel a tiny bit better than yesterday, and steady progress is all that I or anyone else should expect.

We head out driving towards a busy day. Jayden has done a fabulous job of organizing our priorities and even made a list for "if we have time." Since we technically don't even have a full two days, it will be exciting to see what all we can accomplish, especially since I'm not an equal partner.

Throughout the day and into the evening, I nearly smother him with appreciation. With each task I scratch through, I see how important it is to map out my day. A strong back is what he offers, and it's exactly what I need. His willingness to be patient with me, and his desire to help regardless of how much I can do means the world to me, and I'm not really sure how I can do this without him.

"Thanks, man. I really appreciate your help today. I know it's spur of the moment, and I don't deserve it, but really, I can't thank you enough for all you're doing," I say after I bow my head and give thanks over our restaurant-prepared cuisine.

Jayden's face looks funny in response, and I ask what makes him look so contorted.

He reassures me, "Oh, nothing. I just never thought I would see the day you give thanks to a God who both gives and takes away."

I stop eating and remember how I once felt in both battle and here at home. Knowing my own hatred, I can see how this would be surprising.

"It's just cool to see such a drastic change," he continues. "That's all. Oh and remember, Casey, everyone falls short, just so you know."

I look into my brother's compassionate face, and I have so much to learn about being a Christian. It's not weak to speak of your problems but wise to seek out council. His words are healing, as Proverbs suggests, and I plan to one day extend another the same inspiration. I haven't forgotten my assignment in passing on the Bible, but I pray that when I do I, too, am seasoned in my delivery and can make another spirit glad.

We wind down our dining, discussing our ideas on where to find the next recipient of the Bible. We throw around many great places, but we both believe it will take more than just the two of us to pull it off. It would be great to have Steven and Jacob involved, and the possibilities in our near future continue to grow.

On the way home, we pass by more than one Christian

church, and before I can get it out of my mouth, Jayden suggests we work on finding a place to worship and grow. I don't know the first thing about searching for a good church, having never really walked in one with true intent. I jot down a new to-do on Jayden's list, and he acknowledges it by nodding his head.

Seeing this gesture stirs me to take the lead. As soon as we make it home, I begin arranging the furniture to free up the extra space we need. My anxiety is dissipating the more I put Steven first, and the distraction from my own problems proves helpful.

After we are done doing what we can in one day, I say goodnight early and plan to store up as much rest as I can before our busy tomorrow. I enter my room, and this time I remove my clothes before getting into to bed.

I walk over to the closet to hang up my jacket, and when I open the door the Night Bar slaps me in the face. A stale emptiness lingers inside the closet, and it reminds me of the filthy nights spent there. Immediately, I begin purging and start taking down what I can do without.

Back and forth to the kitchen trash I go, and Jayden doesn't say a thing but watches my coming and going intently. I think for sure with the second black bag of clothing he sees that he will ask what I'm doing, but he doesn't. I make one final pass by and decide to make it simple for him.

"I need a new wardrobe."

He shrugs his shoulders and says, "Okay," giving me another reason to love his easy-going ways. I don't have to explain what's happening inside nor do I feel the pressure to divulge. The important thing is that I'm doing away with all that doesn't fit my new life, and while it may seem confusing to him it makes complete sense to me.

When I'm done doing what I can, I close my door and with it, a chapter of my life. Anxiety over tiny reminders is closer to gone than it was before, and what is left can't be helped. I lie down and take another look at the things we accomplished and what is still left to do.

Today is a success, and the more victory I see, the easier it is to rest. I grab the Bible laying on my nightstand, and I begin reading its words all over again. It's the one thing I can never forget.

My alarm wakes me at 6:00 AM sharp, and there is no use trying to snooze my way through the hour. Steven will be here this afternoon, and we still need to clean up and stock the fridge. My body is sore from the activity from yesterday, but I proceed to my knees and perform my ritual requests for help before I do anything more.

This morning hardly feels any different than the rest of my recent mornings, but I do admit it's easier to accept my responsibility today. I'm not secretly arguing my way out of my obligations, but talking myself into them instead.

"Casey, you can do this," I coach myself.

Water heaters are a great gift from God. The steaming shower unlocks every tense muscle I have, and I stand under the heat until I can no longer tolerate it. My skin is bright red, but it's a good burn, and I wipe down the mirror to see how bad it is. It's pleasing that my reflection does not scare me today. I'm a color that looks alive, and this is the second difference within an hour. I'm hopeful to see more.

I dry off and my positivity fades. I remember that I'll need to tell Steven about my recent behavior, and I hate having to go through this again. Playing the tape forward even more, I'll have to clear things up with Jacob, too. He is also due an explanation, and there is no way around it. My only break is that mom can wait until after Thanksgiving. I won't ruin her day's expectations on purpose.

I brush my teeth and tap Jayden's doorway to let him know I'm out of the shower. I get dressed in a hurry and head to the kitchen to feed myself. Jayden is already in the process of blending a lumpy green shake that I'll bet money is for me. I can't break the news to him that I think his concoction needs work, so I'm in for another semi-nauseating morning. To my relief, the toaster pops up and bagels for breakfast sound delicious.

Over our semi-healthy meal, Jayden and I discuss the order in which we think it's best to knock out what is on our agendas. The grocery store wins for first place, followed by a quick clean. Then we are off to stand in line at the airport. It sounds simple enough, but things never seem to work out exactly as planned.

Halfway through the day, I sit down and take a break. Everything is on track, and we are making excellent time. The only procrastinating is in my desire to talk to Steven. Our big discussion keeps harassing me, and the more it does the worse my nerves get.

It borders on obnoxious, but I don't really know how to get rid of this stupid, repetitive thinking on my own. I suppose not getting myself into a predicament like this to begin with is a smart idea, but it doesn't help me to know this now. I needed to know it back then.

It's frustrating, and I puff my hostility without reserve. I resume my cleaning methods, hoping the vacuum cleaner does a better job of hushing the ridiculousness of it all. Jayden sees my anxiety and walks over to our stereo. He turns the radio on loud enough for the neighbors to hear, but I'm happy about his bright idea.

He looks over at me with a mock-serious face and strokes his broom like the acoustic guitar it isn't. His humor tickles me, and I laugh out loud when I use the vacuum as a microphone. We are naturals, and his decision to rock on carries me through the rest of the afternoon.

Wrapping things up before we walk out the door, I look

back to make sure everything is perfect. We are both so eager I don't want to overlook something simple. We stand in the entryway of our apartment and seeing our ideas for a third roommate come together so nicely, Jayden puts his fist in the air; I take it as a mutual understanding of a job well-done.

It really doesn't look bad with the freestanding closet we bought yesterday and extra shelves and storage space. I'm happy that men are more readily excused for poor decorating than women.

The next thing out of my mouth is, "If he doesn't like it, I'll just blame it on you," and it slips out too easily.

Jayden is quick to tell me, "It figures," and our mutual joking picks up where it left off. I lock the door behind us, and we head towards the airport.

On the way, discussion gets pretty deep. I don't know much about religion, but I'm quickly learning that not everyone believes the same thing. Jayden encourages me to do research on the churches in the local area before we decide to attend one of them, and I agree that I do indeed need to avoid conflicting ideas.

It's encouraging having him by my side to help guide me in my elementary thinking. I can easily see myself just plopping into a pew of any old church, just to be in the company of fine people like Jayden and Sarah. I wouldn't have a clue that it could possibly warp the fresh concepts I've just learned.

To my surprise, Jayden admits his failure to keep his own personal relationship with Christ where it should be. I don't see where he lacks much of anything, but it must be there if he is willing to share.

Hearing that my story inspires him to grow closer to God makes having suffered what I did not sting as badly. It actually gives me ideas on how to share with Steven. I appreciate the final minutes before seeing our friend arrive, and I collect as much courage from our conversation to take with me as I can.

Since 9/11, the airport security is much stricter than it once was, so we post up near the baggage claim and wait to see our friend. It doesn't take long before his oversized frame stands out among the crowd, and his pride in being a Marine sets him apart from the rest.

He is wearing a Corps t-shirt, and something we can count on is that we won't be mugged on the way out. He is one huge, Southern, cornbread-fed boy if I've ever seen one. I forget how much we keep in shape over there, and a bit of unwanted jealousy creeps into my thinking.

As soon as he recognizes our faces, the kid hidden within him comes alive, and he jogs the rest of the way to greet us. Nearly mowing me over, he wraps his thick arms around me and suffocates the strength I've built up. It's not that I'm scared of Steven and what he can do with his physical body, but it's how much I'll disappoint his gentle spirit.

Pulling away, I don't think I've seen someone so excited since I was a child. Worry crosses my face, and I spot Jayden peaking past him to check on me. Steven going on about how thrilled he is to be here is only making honesty more difficult. I shrug the impulse to run and make a joke instead.

"In all seriousness, dude, I don't know if our couch is big enough to hold you."

We all find the humor in my comment, as it must have been exactly what Jayden was thinking, and laughter fills the air around us. Picking on our new arrival doesn't last long. Steven chimes in quickly like we were never separated and sends a slug to my upper left triceps, nearly knocking me off balance. I whimper out loud and the roar of what's funny grows. I deserve the embarrassment. I should pick on people my own size.

This jumpstarts the beginning of something new, and seeing how comfortable we all are together gives me slightly more enthusiasm about sharing my condition. We collect his bags and head out, talking about way too many topics at one time. His military slang that is still fresh provokes the longing I have for my past, but instead of sulking I choose joy for this occasion.

Steven's deep voice matches his dominant physique, but when he begins to open up it rings insecure. I assume that it's from never being able to call a place home for longer than a few years.

When he starts in with how much he appreciates us allowing him to stay for a while, I make light of his burden and declare, "Well, it's absolutely no problem. We were getting ready to hire a maid anyway. Whatever you do, don't forget I like my steaks medium rare, and Jayden likes his a little more burnt."

Another punch is thrown in my direction from the backseat, but I'm much quicker in dodging his attempts at shutting me up this time. My truck is full, and I lean towards the window as far as I can to get without jumping out.

"Big Sissy" is what he calls me, and I don't have a problem with it in the least. I don't think he realizes the power behind his punch. I'm not going to stand by and wait for his hammer of a fist to connect again. In a week's time, I'll look like a spotted mutt from all the bruising, and I need all of my body's energy working on the aches I already have.

I laugh at his name-calling. It's fairly appropriate. Steven outranks us, having put in two more years, and he's famous for giving people a tough time. I appreciate it more than he knows. I just pray that these insults don't turn serious when he finds out I became a junkie for awhile.

We wait in a long line trying to leave the airport parking lot. The scuttlebutt is interesting, and it looks like talking about what he's leaving behind seems to help him adjust. Every so often I turn around and face him directly to listen, and I catch the same overly cautious reactions to the things around him as I had when I first came out.

I smile and tell him it gets better. He doesn't ask to what I'm referring and carries on with the latest news of our friends out east. Not much is different from a daily grind perspective, but Steven does say that no one has forgotten what we did.

"They're still talking about y'all's crazy Geronimo out of that window. Y'all are regular heroes over there. I should get your autographs while I gotcha. I'll send them over on a snapshot for twenty bucks a piece. We can split what we make. What do you say?"

I look at Jayden and our pride swells. I offer to hit Steven and his Southern accent, but I quickly recant. If I wound his mouth, I might not have the chance of hearing him say this again. It's nice to be remembered for your guts.

We catch up two years in about an hour, and no one is tired of talking yet. We ask all kinds of things and while listening to Jayden pour out so many need-to-knows over dinner, I realize I'm not the only one who feels a loss. Soon the questions change direction. They're aimed at me, and I fumble for the correct answer.

"So, Casey, what do you do in your spare time?" Steven asks casually, having no clue of the response that's in store for him.

Since I'm skinnier than he has ever seen, offering that I work out is not an option. I could try telling him I run, but the first time he sees me ready to crumble after only a half mile, it will be evident that I'm a liar. It's the perfect lead in to an answer I have no choice but to give.

I look over at Jayden, and he casually picks up his napkin to wipe his face. He clears his throat and raises his eyebrows.

He asks if I'm sure this is the right time or not. I don't know if it is, but I don't think there will be another opportunity where I'm asked so directly what I'm involved in.

I set down my freshly poured glass of iced tea and wipe my face from anything that may be distracting. I don't know where to start.

"Look, Steven," I say, "I wanted to talk to you about something that you may notice once we get back home and into a routine. I don't have a lot of energy right now, and I move pretty slowly, but it's getting better every day, and I just wanted you to know for knowledge's sake that I'm okay. Don't worry, it's not catching or anything, but I just want to put it out there so you're not caught off guard."

"You sick?" Steven's question is very simple and full of concern. I wish my answer could match it, but it can't. I consider how I can best explain what it is that ails me, but words are not my gift.

"Well, you could say I was for a while, but I ..." I hesitate for a second then just stop procrastinating the truth any longer. It's stupid to drag out the inevitable. "Well, to tell you the truth, it's nothing more than me withdrawing from a whole heck of a lot of street drugs and late nights.

"But like I said, don't worry, I found Jesus and addiction is not catching or anything unless you choose to hate life as you know it and use dope to avoid reality every single day. Then there is a possibility that you might become infected, but even then you have to keep on keeping on."

Jayden's mouth falls open, and he nearly spits his food across the table. Immediately, Steven and I perk up, and the crowd nearby is staring. He looks like he is choking on the earlier words I couldn't bring myself to say, but now that it's out there and on the table, he is not the one I have to worry about.

Jayden coughs a few more times and brings his fist to his

chest in order to pat down the nerves that are giving him so much trouble. I look to Steven to read what I can from his facial expression, but I have no clue what he's thinking.

We both wait in awkward silence for him to speak, and for a solid minute he doesn't say a thing, only chews his food. I prepare myself for an intentional blow to my jaw, but it never comes, and it makes me worry even more. I assume he is trying to digest what I've said, but when he speaks I change my mind.

"Ya big dummy," he says without further delay. "What did you go and do that for, boy? You know how stupid that is. That's by far got to be the dumbest thing I've ever known you to do. You know better than that. Drugs? Really?"

Steven's face bunches into several tiny wrinkles that are indistinguishable one from another. It's clear that he is not pleased with this news. I'm also not happy about the way it came out but better now, bluntly, instead of a smoothed over, half-story later.

I watch Steven as he takes out his aggression on the poor vegetables lying on his plate. One by one he stabs the green beans, and never once do I take my eyes off of his weapon. He finally looks back up at me and points his fork like a dagger in my direction.

"You're over it, right?" His fork is a threat and aimed directly at my heart. I relax for the first time since he arrived.

"Ya, man. I'm over it."

Steven lowers his head back down towards his food and continues to eat while shaking his head. Who can want more than that? I let out a huge sigh of relief, and Jayden seconds this motion with a large exhale of his own.

"I half thought you were going to stab me," I say as a joke while coupling my comment with a snicker, but Steven's response cuts me short.

"I still might while you're laughing."

He looks mean, and I quit smiling immediately. As soon as I do, Jayden and Steven burst into laughter. While I can't scold them for making fun of me, I'm glad the moment for sharing what I had to is over. I throw my napkin down in the center of the table as a warning of my own for them to stop, but it only makes matters worse and laughter is contagious, so I join them. Steven will fit in nicely. I decide to keep the rest of the evening light from here on out and bring up Thanksgiving as a peace offering.

"Mom wants us all to come to Colorado Springs for Thanksgiving. I wasn't sure if you had plans already or not, but I included you in the head count I gave her. I hope you don't mind. I can always cancel your spot if you're not interested, but since you will be here I figured you might like to go with us. Mom loves the company and she's one outstanding turkey dresser."

Steven barely lets me finish my statement. "Seriously? Like, a real, home-cooked turkey and gravy, hot meal, prepared on purpose, for us, so that we can eat it, all together, around a table, as much as we want kind of Thanksgiving?"

I chuckle.

"Well, heck ya, count me in. Can I call her 'mom'?" Steven's excitement and appreciation of things I take for granted removes whatever weird thinking that still lingers. His Southern accent draws me away from myself and into his history that will no longer dictate his future. He has a family now, and we are it.

We finish our food and wrap up our conversation with what he might like to do on his first Saturday in New York City. We offer up suggestions from Times Square to the Statue of Liberty, but when "a Coney dog in Central Park" is his choice, we understand him still thinking about food. Good flavor stuns the mind into remembering what is great about being an American.

Neither one of us blames him or argues against it. Hot dogs are a favorite meal for Jayden and me, too. We actually ate so many when we first moved here that we were sick of them by the end of the month, and it kept us away for three more, easy.

We agree to satisfy his hunger after a morning of discussing the details that I skipped over tonight. My new project needs explaining and all the help it can get. I'm hoping Steven is as generous with his time as Jayden is with his.

Show and tell will be interesting, and a good meal in the park will be well-deserved after lending an ear for so long. I have to remind myself to remain sensitive to his needs to unwind and settle in. I'm on fire, and it's hard to control these new feelings. I know my story is unique and requires a certain amount of mental commitment to process. I don't want to overwhelm him with too much to think about at one time.

We head home, still chatting about how we're going to get to Colorado. Jayden and Steven prefer a road trip to view our country's little-seen backdrops, but I'm still in the thick of withdrawal and wish to get there the quickest and least painful way possible. I can't wait until I'm back to normal and rotating inside of a crammed truck for 26 hours straight sounds fun again.

We arrive back home and all grab a piece of luggage to carry in with us. The wind is chilly, and somehow my attention turns to Steven. I remember my own touchdown and all that came with it. The acclimating alone is enough to exhaust you. There are new climates, new smells, new people, and new sounds. Your situation changes every few seconds, and in order to keep secure you almost feel the need to withdraw before you have even given anything a deserving chance.

I place my hand on the backside of Steven's shoulder and

remind him that he is not alone. There is no special course for this moment. No one teaches us how to come back. We have a farewell and a new beginning inside of the same 24 hours, and it's a great deal for one day.

We don't carry an operations manual to calculate if we are doing things right in order to maintain new relationships or keep proper distance from the old. There is no gauge to reassure us that we are doing anything right.

Knowing Steven had no real example to follow growing up only increases my curiosity on how he processes his new journey. I wonder if God grants him extra help for having been abandoned for so long. He looks at me, and I sense his appreciation. As long as Steven knows I'm only one step behind him, he can move forward with confidence.

We head up to our apartment one in front of another, and it feels right. We unlock the door, and I realize that I'm no longer an active Marine but an active Christian. I don't have a mission on foreign soil, but I do have one here, a very large one that is more important than all others combined. It's my job and duty to help someone in the dark find their way to the light. My responsibility is great, and this will all be impossible without God.

"So, Steven," Jayden says, "are you glad to be stateside?"

Steven answers Jayden's question on our way in with little hesitancy.

"Well, it's different. It's been a minute since I've been back home. I mean, this really isn't home either, down south is. I just don't have anyone down there since my foster brother passed last year due to cancer. I'm more or less looking for a new place and figured I could use the two of you as a lift to get to wherever it is I'm supposed to go. I guess I'm feeling my way around until something fits. I really appreciate you guys bridging the gap, if you know what I mean."

Piling in our apartment, I look over at Jayden and him at me. "Anytime!" we say together. Steven's excitement interrupts us before we can say anything more to reassure him of his welcome here.

"Dude, this is awesome! I'm going to assume that this is my room?"

We step into the living room, and I collapse into our leather recliner before I offer him any answer to appease him. I don't conceal my fatigue well, and Steven and Jayden kindly ignore what they see. I use my feet to remove my shoes and lean back as far as the chair will take me.

"Ya, man, this is your room," I answer him as I place my hands behind my neck for more support.

I leave him to his own exploring. I try not to pry or pay too much attention, but watching him is fascinating. I look around with him, and our pad is impressive. Everything is neat but macho in style. Marine posters hang on the walls with team banners in the corners.

For anyone's intrigue, a display of old Army knives can be found alongside a row of model airplanes on the top shelf of our entertainment center. Jayden's new hobby of miniature shipbuilding brings more than a few odd nautical pieces to the next shelf, and what you see after that is our pride in our country.

If you continue to follow it down any further, in the center you will find a media station after any man's own heart. Below are books on every subject from history to cars, and if you look closely my father's antique harmonica is hiding somewhere. Pictures of our brothers in the Far East line its sides; it's a custom cabinet worth admiring. Jayden and I have a habit of collecting things from our overnight adventures, and a stand altogether separate is dedicated to remembering those events.

Steven's thrill at seeing our place is comical when he runs

around in circles in the middle of the room, declaring, before he has seen the rest, that he indeed has the best room in the house. I can't help but laugh at him and his childlike response.

"So let me get this straight," he says. "I have the biggest TV, the best surround sound, my own personal library, I'm closest to the kitchen, there is a bathroom within eight feet, I've got a sofa, love seat, and recliner in my room, and you're worried it won't be big enough because, why, exactly? It's perfect and I, my brothers, am a king."

Steven declares his majesty and finally plops down dead center of his new fold-out throne. Jayden joins us and also finds pleasure in Steven's outburst.

"Dude, this is what I call a nice place. I bet you have no problem with the ladies. Either one of you seeing anyone?"

Jayden and I laugh again at Steven's enthusiastic reaction. He is excited, and we know the feeling. Somewhere between unsure and sure he made a decision to accept things as they are, and his choice to make the best of what he gets is evidence that attitude makes a difference.

With conversation heading in a direction that I'm no good at, I sit for only a few more minutes before I excuse myself for the rest of the night. It's early but neither say anything, and I leave them discussing what fun can be found in walking distance.

I'm tired and as soon as I make it behind my door, I slouch into a more appropriate position to accommodate the twinge my back won't release. I grunt in taking off my clothes like it's the hardest obstacle in the world, and my bed welcomes me even more sweetly than it did last night.

I lie down flat on my back and pull my covers over me. I close my eyes to a seriously long day, but the low-watt bulb in the lamp on my bedside table is more offensive than I expect. I huff in having to sit up like it's someone else's fault they left it on, and as soon as I flip the toggle switch I slam my head back into the pillow.

I lie without moving while my mind slowly gives up its authority. Shutting down is much easier when I actually give my body a reason to rest. My mind roams from one thing to another, and with the earlier suggestion of women it settles on Sarah. I wonder how she was approached in becoming involved in my story and if it took much persuasion at all for her to agree.

The kind of hope she carries I doubt can be orchestrated, and the light she brought to my wade through dark times makes her someone for me to never forget. I doubt I'll ever have the opportunity in this big city to see her again, so I just ask the Lord to bless her as part of my final contribution for today.

I'm semi-conscious when I hear the juicer's motor start blending in our kitchen. Even in my limited state, I smile and am glad Steven's here to satisfy Jayden's need to be healthy. I drift off and do not wake until early morning.

The clock reads 2:55 AM, and I'm anxious for some reason. I don't know why I shake but I do. I open my eyes, and everything is what it should be for this time. The dark is quiet, and nothing is disturbed but my soul.

I swallow to clear my throat and realize I'm parched. I feel around on my nightstand for a water bottle, but I didn't make any provisions for thirst before bed. I hate to wake up Steven on accident, but I have to pass by his palace in order to get a drink. I feel dehydrated. I get up and move quietly past him. I don't make much noise, but Steven asks me if I'm alright as soon as I go by.

"Just thirsty," I tell him, and he rolls onto his side like it's nothing unusual to be woken up. I pour a glass of milk instead of water, hoping it's more filling, and return to my room with extra just in case it's not. I crawl back into bed and lie there, no more settled than before. I review the day in my mind, and it seems like telling Steven the truth would have taken care of this kind of anticipation.

I look over at the clock again, and it's almost 4:00 AM. I'm drifting in and out of sleep, but I'm not resting well. I blame it on my body's chemistry trying to readjust to the changes I've made, but this conclusion doesn't quite explain why my heart weighs so much.

I talk to God, since He's the only one up, and ask Him what the problem is, but I don't hear any response. When I look at the clock again, it shows another hour has passed, and I sigh.

At 6:01 AM I get up, regardless of who is awake. I'm not near as stiff this morning as I'm used to being, but shifting all night prevents the discomfort I get from lying in the same place too long.

I sit up and stretch out. I hit my knees out of habit next and collect all I need for a shower after that. I wash away as much as I can from an awkward night and get on with how I need to prepare for surrendering the Bible over to a new owner.

Getting Steven on board will be a third pair of hands and probably a desperately needed set. I can't imagine who the Lord has in mind to receive the book next, but I hope I recognize them when I see them.

I pick up my security, and my fondness for its used leather might present a problem in handing it over to someone else. I hope it makes the same difference for them as it does for me and that they take the commitment in passing it on to another as seriously as I do.

I make my bed and walk out, carrying the object of the day's show and tell lesson. I sneak past Steven a little better than I did last night, but when I crack the first egg he comes in to join my breakfast preparations.

It doesn't take long for Steven to notice the Bible laying on the kitchen table and an even shorter time for him to pick it up and find the words written in the back. I allow him to finish what he's doing and wait for the next predictable question.

When it comes out, I casually begin sharing how everything transpired over the course of the last few weeks while I continue to cook. Jayden walks in shortly after I begin, sits down at the table, and listens for a second time to the story that changed my life. Never once does he show a lesser interest for something he's already heard.

As I make my way through the week I spent on the floor, the smell of seared pork cuts through the air, and I hope it has the same alluring effect on Steven as it does on me. Trying to win his allegiance through his belly may not be the most ethical thing to do, but I'm just starting out, and I really need his support in this endeavor. After eating, Steven calls me out on my blatant attempt to use his gut to gain access to his favor. I don't deny the accusation.

"Well, what do you say? Are you in or are you out?" I ask what I'm hoping the bacon has already persuaded for me, and his response is golden.

"Well, if that book did all that for you, there is a strong chance that it can do that for somebody else. It's not typical, but I smell an adventure. Count me in."

He winks at me, and I've never been so excited to receive this kind of gesture from a male. I now have two extra set of hands, and if I can manage to gain Jacob's allegiance, I'll have a very good chance of following Dan's lead and succeed in passing on the Bible.

We finish breakfast off with lighter discussion, and it perks up our morning. Steven has a great sense of humor, and he takes every opportunity he can to give me a hard time about my life choice. I chime in, welcoming his form of punishment, and it's no time before I see through the eyes of another how complicated I chose to make my life.

Watching Jayden respond to him making light of a tough time allows me to see how much on edge I made him in the midst of my using. These new insights are painful in a way but make my determination not to use, grow.

I clear the table, and the absence of leftovers makes it fairly easy to clean. Steven's final comment that Jayden is probably starving after drinking all that healthy stuff makes all three of us chuckle. Jayden brings on his revenge by placing a full glass in each of our hands and telling us to drink up before we start our day. It seems the joke is on us.

Steven acts as though he has been stabbed in the chest, but even during his fake death, kills his cup in two extremely large gulps. What's bad is that he already made mention of it not tasting horrible, and that is all Jayden needs to continue in his campaign. It takes me quite a bit longer, but I do as I'm told.

When I finish the secret formula, Jayden brings up Sunday's agenda. There are so many churches to choose from that he makes a list and begins reading off their names. Steven declares he is perfectly comfortable with any of the long-named churches we mention and that the choice is ours. Apparently, growing up in the south, everyone's parent, grandparent, aunt, or uncle—or in his case, foster parent—attends church at least one Sunday a month and every holiday no matter what. The idea of Jesus as Savior is not a foreign one to him at all.

"Whatever y'all pick is good," he says.

That's all he contributes to the decision-making process, and I have a feeling conversation went fairly deep last night after I went to bed. I further Sunday's itinerary when I offer to take Steven and Jayden to the infamous coffee shop after church.

"It's about twenty minutes or so from here. It will stretch your thinking when you see it. Jayden hasn't been there yet, either, so it will be the first time for you both. I figure you will need to know exactly where it is if we plan to lead someone."

"Man this is kinda deep," Steven cuts in. "So let me get this straight. This Bible is being passed around by a bunch of ex-Marines?"

It's a very good question, so I try and clarify his thinking.

"Well, service men, for sure. I think it just started between two Marines. This particular coffee shop I mentioned is where people always seem to wind up at in the end, so I'm assuming it may have something to do with where it all began. I have a hunch that it's owned by the family of one of the dead Marines, but I can't be certain of that without prying, and it isn't absolutely necessary for me to know.

"I do know that they know something, or at least someone does, to allow all the letters to be posted without argument. The place contains a wall of appreciation from those who were once a temporary owner of the Bible. Once you see it and read some the words of these men, you will understand for yourself how serious this all really is."

I pause and wait for a response to my offer in taking them by there tomorrow. Both of them say yes and agree that it's essential in conducting any plan that will work.

"Great. As soon as you get acquainted with the layout of the place, we can start working on where to find this guy we're supposed to help. I have a couple ideas of where the lost hang out but nothing guaranteeing a military man."

I bare my beginner leadership skills, and Steven chimes in to rescue me.

"Oh, dude, that's not a problem at all. Have you been to the local VA? Tons of folks there need help. Many of them are just barely getting by. It's kind of sad, actually. I've never been to this one up here, but I'm pretty sure they all look the same on the inside. Sick, wounded, and dying. If that doesn't qualify them for the book, I don't know what does."

His answer is brilliant, and I'm kind of ashamed that I didn't think of it myself. He is right. It's not hard to find people who need help because we all do over one thing or another.

"Hey, that's a great idea, but how are we going to pick who? The VA is packed," I say and Steven explains.

"Well, I didn't say I know all that now. I guess you'll just have to ask God to pick and let you know, friend. Besides, I'm just the dude helping you to carry out the plan. I never said I was any good at making them big decisions." Steven's Southern drawl tickles me, and his simple honesty is a pleasure to work with.

I grin, acknowledging his refusal to take the lead, and the fact that he is so funny makes me think about using his accent to attract conversation at the hospital. I catch myself thinking about taking advantage of him twice in one day and grin again. This will surely be a funny sight to see Steven laying on his heritage thicker than it already is. I can't wait.

"But if that don't work, they've got them halfway houses, shelters, churches, missions, soup kitchens, YMCAs." He goes on slowly. "They all have or know someone who needs help."

Steven comes back with even more leads, and I stop him right there.

"Whoa, slow down, we haven't made it through the hospital yet. How do you—" I begin to ask him how he knows about all of these kinds of places, but I catch myself before I insert my foot in my mouth. I'm glad I do.

"What's that?" Steven asks about the sentence I fail to

end, but I save myself and begin another.

"How do you wanna get to the park? It's cold out, but if you two are going to make me run I won't wear a heavy coat."

"Oh, you'll still need a heavy coat. Those bones lack the meat to keep anybody warm."

Steven's quick wit forces me to land a blow directly to his forearm, and I turn and run to the door. My fist lands hard and on such a sold surface that it scares me. I don't want to be on the wrong end of his retaliation. Laughter fills the apartment and "Big Sissy" looks like it's becoming Steven's new affectionate term for me.

"At least I'm a fast, Big Sissy!" I yell back, and I can see in my brother's eyes as they round the corner from the kitchen that they conspired in my absence and are now ready to tag team me. I turn only a third serious and warn them.

"Hey, that's not fair!"

Before I can get out anything further, they tackle me. They slam me up against the door, and being wedged between two rocks makes it pretty difficult to free myself. I push, pull, kick, press, and tug. I don't even gain an inch. I think about pulling Jayden's short hair for comic relief, but I can't get to him through the headlock I'm now placed in.

"Uncle, uncle!" I burst into laughter, and I can feel the blood being blocked from leaving my face. I'm laughing but I'm really about to pass out, so I tap out using the front door, and Steven finally releases his death grip on me.

"Man, don't you know I'm a recovering addict? It has to qualify as a handicap or something."

I'm quick to find an excuse for my weakness, and Steven shuts the door to any special advance start I'll ever get.

"It don't count when you made yourself sick."

I look back at him and see a few silver sparks around his

face. *"Touché,* brother, *touché."*

I give him the only right response and in regaining proper blood flow, I notice we all look a mess. Steven, of course, blames me for wrinkling his new shirt, and Jayden fixes his own collar from a two-fold twist. When we finally put ourselves back together, Steven answers the question I asked to begin with.

"Just for that, we're going to run there and back."

I wince over the painful news and start to wonder if God didn't send Steven on purpose to literally help whip me back into shape. I mumble under my breath, thanking God for His not-so-secret attempts to mold me. Everyone but me leaves the apartment eager for our outdoor trek.

It doesn't take long before I fall behind, and Steven and Jayden slow their pace out of camaraderie. I appreciate their loyalty, and by the time we get there I've exhausted all of the energy I stored up sleeping. Out of sympathy, they pick a bench and we aim for it, but Steven stops before I can enjoy the intentional break.

"Whoa, what is that I'm smelling?" he asks, and like dogs, Jayden and I lift our noses into the air to catch the scent that stops him in his tracks.

We find nothing unusual, and before we can ask specifically what he's referring to, he points out a street vender standing along the sidewalk in front of a large, steaming metal cart. The overweight man's line is long, and Jayden and I acknowledge his curiosity as being well-founded.

"Oh, that. Yes, that is one of the greatest things about this city. It's one of the few pleasures I extend to myself, no matter the fat content. Did you want to eat now? It's only ten-thirty. If you wait thirty minutes, you can claim it as your lunch."

Jayden waits for Steven to respond, but when he turns his back on us and heads in the opposite direction, we know what his answer is. Steven picks up his speed, and we have to two-step it in order to catch up with him. Out of curiosity, he goes directly to the front of the line. We laugh knowing that he is far from Southern hospitality.

"I've got five bucks says that nice school teacher-looking lady lets him have it."

Before I can seal our deal, we hear Steven get the cursing of his life. His big, bold physique doesn't scare the tiny, northern woman at all. She continues to shout for him to wait his own turn as he heads back towards the end of the line, with his tail tucked between his legs, to where we are already standing, waiting patiently for his return.

"Shut up!" Steven whispers as he falls smoothly into line behind us.

Both Jayden and I keep our faces straight forward, trying not to burst into laughter, but we can't contain it when Steven whispers, "Dang, she must be hungry, right?"

Our intrusive cackling invades the entire lineup, including the not-so-nice schoolmarm in front. We receive the typical New York City response, including rolling eyes, sighs, and judgmental gestures for invading their personal ear space.

Steven, of course, waves like the out-of-towner he is, and when they all turn their backs on him he really does look confused. Jayden and I place our hands over our mouths in order to quiet the level of excitement coming from them, but it doesn't help much. We finally quit once we are next in line, and Steven breaks in front of me when I turn my head to notice something unusual.

I can only see her from the side, but I would know that face from anywhere. My angel isn't but 100 feet from me, holding the hand of a tiny, beautiful, toddler-aged little girl. Her bright, yellow pigtails shine in the sun, and although it's chilly I feel the warmth of concern.

A mundane voice breaks my concentration, and I look

away for only a split second to tell him to give me the same thing Jayden ordered. I look back at what I glimpsed out of the corner of my eye, and when I do I'm sure of the panic I feel.

I jump out of the line and out of the way of the people who are blocking me. I yell as I run, but the barking dogs, acoustic guitar, distant car horns, construction machinery, and kids chanting school yard rhymes all block me and drown out the impact my warning is meant to give.

I try again, but they both seem absolutely oblivious to what is beside them. I stretch my legs as far as they will separate without them folding from underneath me, and I run what seems like a mile-long distance, under the circumstances. I can't get there fast enough.

I'm so close that I can hear their voices, but while engrossed in one another's presence they are completely unaware of the danger standing so close to them. I scream Sarah's name as I gain proximity, hoping to disturb them both from their naivety, but neither responds as quickly as they should.

I can hear my brothers yelling my name behind me in the distance, but there is nothing that can or will stop me from trying to save them. Sarah's eyes finally meet mine, and she reads that something is extremely wrong, but she has waited too long to hear me.

The gun fires, and they are not safe. Screams ring out, and those standing hit the ground out of their own instinct to save themselves. The young girl on Sarah's side reaches for protection in her arms, leaving them both exposed and too easy of a target.

In my peripheral vision, as I leap in front of the two I'm trying to protect, I can see the gunman threaten Jimmy Nix until his final end. Two bullets are fired from the gangster's 9mm hand gun. One rips through Jimmy's mind, and as I

look into the blood-stained dress of the young child, failure
stings me. I'm too late. Her moans for her mother hurt me
to hear, and as I reach for them both, I can't breathe or stand.

I fall, gasping for air along with hope. A hole in the center
of me begins to fill. Time spills forward in slow motion as
blood begins to pour out over the surface of my chest. I
reach out and cough, trying to clear the bubbles that irritate
my throat. The tart taste of pain hits me hard, and it brings
me to the ground. I cough again. It isn't helping remove
whatever is stuck in my airway.

Sarah bends down with her wailing child to check on me,
and her trembling is notable. Through quivering lips she
tells me to hang on, but she is pulled away from me within
a second. The convulsions don't stop, and I realize it's me
who is shaking so badly.

Jayden is the next thing I see, and I notice that his concentration is largely split when he hovers over me. I can hear
commotion disturbing the crowd, but I can't see Steven anywhere. Jayden evaluates me and immediately takes off his
jacket and removes his shirt. I start to speak, and bright red
blood spits into the air, tainting the taste in the roof of my
mouth even further. I'm warned.

"Shhhh, Casey. Don't speak. It's bad. This is going to
hurt."

Bending over, he shoves the fabric as far into the wound
as it will possibly allow him to go. I feel the pressure of him
leaning on me, but it's harder to acknowledge the pain than
just fall asleep. His face is close to mine, but I can hardly
make it out.

"Jayden," I try to speak again, but as the words come out
poorly the light in the sky fades, blinding my view with
darkness.

I can still hear, but it's the last sense I have. Sirens in the
distance promise someone is coming to save me, but I'm

not in that much pain anymore. I can't smell anything because I can't breathe. I'm dying.

"Casey! Casey! Oh God, please help him!"

I hear the plea of my best friend beside me, and I agree with his direction. Up is a nice place to go, and as my body feels like it can float I cease to comprehend.

CHAPTER NINE

I would say I feel like I'm trying to drown but am being kept alive with the bare minimum amount of oxygen it requires to survive. My hearing is what I notice first. A constant monitor beeps around me in a pattern with a much longer and even more annoying one accompanying it. The constant sound of something decompressing and wisping by my face makes me feel the need to shoo it away, but I'm not quite sure I can move.

I recognize the sounds I hear as those of a hospital, and I try and remember what brings me here. Everything is hazy, but I feel for the texture of my surroundings anyway. My body does not respond to my demand to reassure myself, and I realize that I'm not yet fully awake.

I listen patiently for someone or something familiar. The specific sound I search for is not here yet. My eyes begin to itch, and I blink them in order to remove the irritation aggravating me. As I do, a recognizable voice speaks and breaks the barrier of being all by myself.

"Casey, can you hear me?" I would know my brother's voice anywhere, and he asks me the question again before I've had time to respond. "Casey, can you hear me?"

As I aim to reply, I notice that I can't. Inside of my mouth, my tongue is trapped beneath what feels like ribbed plastic. The tube is invasive, and I try and bite down in order for Jayden to remove it.

"Whoa, whoa, whoa, slow down, Casey. Stop. I'm right here. You can't speak. Don't try. But if you open your eyes you should be able to see me."

I strongly disagree with his method of communicating, but I have no other choice and Jayden has never given me poor advice, so I listen. I concentrate and open my eyes with the intent to see only him, but when I do I'm impressed by the large staff surrounding us. It looks like mainly nurses in worn scrubs and their assistants aiding them, but as they notice that I'm conscious, the large number dwindles.

"Casey?" Jayden grabs my attention quickly. He can probably see the questions already beginning to form in my eyes. I look back at him, expecting him to answer every single one of them.

"Don't try and talk. You're on a ventilator to help you breathe. You were shot in the chest. Do you remember that?" Jayden pauses in order to allow me time to think, but I'm impatient to know what's happening to me.

I just stare at him, clueless. I can see him trying to gauge whether or not I understand.

"Do you remember, Casey? Do you remember getting shot in the park?" I look away from him and towards the drab ceiling above, trying to find the moment he is referring to, but it's still not clear. Bits and pieces of strange events present themselves but no full length account that I can understand or make any sense of.

"Casey?" I give Jayden my attention again. "We were in the park. You, me, and Steven. You saw something no one else did. You took care of it. Remember?"

I stare into Jayden, wishing to see from his perspective what he's trying to remind me of, but I'm getting frustrated with myself. I look back at the ceiling for answers. They are not there. I scold myself. *Think, Casey. What happened?* I question myself, trying to encourage the images to form one big picture that I can get, but it just isn't happening for me. I'm getting scared.

"Casey?"

Warm tears swell in my eyes and fall into the base of my ear. I look back at my brother and beg for the memory I can't remember. In a very calm voice, he reassures me that everything is going to be okay without actually saying the words. He works with me and tells me more of what I wish to know.

"Rosemary is going to be okay."

As the name of no one I know comes out of his mouth, I'm completely, without question, at a loss. My mind is not getting better but worse. I have no idea who Rosemary is, and all I can do is narrow my brow and tell him so.

"Rosemary is the little girl you took the bullet for. She and a young woman named Sarah."

Immediately, like a flood, information pours back into my mind with the recognition of this precious name. Jayden can see that it triggers something and continues with his update, now that it looks as though I can actually process what he is saying correctly.

"Casey, you saved their lives. You slowed down and changed the path of the bullet. It hit you square in the chest, then bounced off your spine. When it did, the change in direction caused it to only nick the girl's right shoulder blade. She will have stitches, a decent scar, and one pretty amazing story to tell when she is graduating high school, fully grown. You're a hero, brother ... all over again."

Before I can beg for any more information, an extremely giant Steven and overly stressed Jacob come barging into the room and interrupt any further progress we can make.

"Don't worry, I got him. I got him!" is all Steven has the chance to say before Jacob pushes past him and gains the closest position next to me that he can get.

"Casey, I called your mom. She's coming in on the red eye. She'll be here as soon as she can but understands if you have to start the surgery without her. She told me to tell you that she loves you with all of her heart and that she is proud of you. To hang in there."

He continues with his own words. "We're all proud of you, Casey. I heard what you did. Not just in the park but in your life. All of it. Jayden told me. It's incredible. We love you. I love you."

The sentiments are appreciated, but the questions that arise as a result keep building. Steven continues with his partial story, and what he says explains why Jayden's face is the only one I remember before apparently passing out.

"And the man who shot you, I took care of him. He may not walk again himself, but I got him, and he's going to pay."

Instantly, Jacob looks to Jayden, Jayden to Steven, and Steven back at me. I'm missing something, and if they don't start talking I'm going to chew my way through this tube in my mouth. The three forget me for a moment and have a silent conversation among themselves. I understand this to be knowledge of something I don't have, and the curiosity is killing me.

What surgery, and what about walking, and how come I can't move my hand and get your attention to tell you to just spit it out already? Hey, listen to me! What's going on?

What's happening? Why can't I move? Why are you guys quiet? Talk to me!

I yell within myself at Jayden, and I swear he hears me subliminally. He moves his hand from the bar beside me, and it disappears. He waits a few seconds and then asks me.

"Casey, can you feel me squeezing your hand? Blink once for yes, twice for no."

I don't feel a thing. I can't tell if he is even touching me at all, so I answer hoping that he will squeeze hard enough that I can feel it the next time. His face falls to the floor, and when it does, I panic. I start blinking with all my might.

Once, twice, three times, four, five, six, answer me! I scream inside.

Jacob tells me to calm down, and Jayden lifts his face from the ground where I suppose he is searching for something. His very calm, controlled voice from earlier returns, but it doesn't settle me like it did the first time he used it. His hand vanishes from my sight again but returns interwoven with mine. I can't feel him, but I know he is touching me. I understand now.

Tears return, and I'm helpless to wipe them from my face. My fear is laying bare with no secret to its depth. No one says a word, but both Jayden and Jacob join me in my sorrow. When I finally collect myself, he takes a rag and wipes my face for me. The fact that he has to do this because I can't makes me cry again. They are all patient with me. As soon as we think I'm done, Jayden continues to tell me what I don't know.

"The doctors repaired the hole in your lungs without problem, but the bullet hit your spine as it passed through, and there are fragments of bone blocking the signals going back and forth from your brain. It has caused serious paralysis. They want to try and repair the damage so that you can have at least some feeling and mobility, but the chances that they will succeed aren't good. They're bad, actually. But they are still willing to try. The choice will be up to you, of course, but know we are here and I'm not leaving you."

I listen to him, but this time it doesn't matter that I'm mute. I couldn't find a word even if I were allowed to speak. All I can do is stare into the space that separates me from God's side and wonder without understanding why He wouldn't just take me if I was going to end up this way.

All I want to do is what You asked me to do. I remind God of our plans for the Bible, and I can't believe that He has just forgotten them. My tears return, but I don't let them fall this time.

"Casey, if it were me, I would try." Jayden gives his opinion, and it's welcome. I would ask for it if I could speak.

"Me, too," Steven and Jacob agree, and it's unanimous. I'll try.

Overhead, I can see a light start blinking and hear pages echo in the hall for someone to get to ICU. I wonder if it's me they are coming to attend to. I'm not sure how I can handle all of this without being able to talk or ask questions.

Jayden tells me, "That's probably the doctor coming to talk with you. He was asked to be notified as soon as you became coherent. He will probably ask you for permission to do the surgery I was telling you about. Just remember, Casey, I'm right here, and I'm not leaving no matter how it all turns out. I'll make Steven carry you around on his back everywhere, if I have to."

Steven wants to laugh, I can tell, but downgrades his chuckle to a nice, smiling agreement.

"Hey, no problems here. I have to keep up these guns somehow."

Like all fine Marines, he flexes his biceps in order to prove his ability. I appreciate their trying to make light of this horrible news, and the fact that they include me without it sounding like major troubles warms my heart.

His reassurances help soothe my insecurity, and when a strange man in a large, white overcoat approaches me without an invite, I assume this is who Jayden was talking about. He steps right to the end of my bed and lifts the blankets from around my feet. He takes out a silver instrument, and what he does with it I don't know. His introduction comes right after he makes this informal assessment. He seems to know my body, and the guys by my side, enough so that he pays them no attention at all.

"Hello, Casey. My name is Doctor Thomas Roy. Do you understand that you are in a hospital ICU due to injuries that you sustained while in the course of an altercation in Central Park? Blink once for yes and twice for no if you understand me."

I blink once, and he looks generally pleased. "And do you know these gentlemen to your right and left?" I blink only once again.

"Now, Jayden here is listed as your emergency contact, and he is who I've been discussing your case with, but I'm asking for your consent to speak freely in front of the other two here that are not listed. Do you authorize these two individuals to hear your medical diagnosis and treatment plan?"

I give him the approval he asks for. "Good. I don't think I could make either one of them leave if I wanted to. Especially the big one. They haven't left the hospital since you arrived."

A slight smile and the first sign of a personality beyond the jacket emerge. I'm grateful, and he goes on to update me about my situation.

"First, I wanted to say on behalf of the little girl's mother, thank you for your courage. As a direct result of what you did, you successfully saved both of their lives and quite possibly many others, as well. They don't make enough of you to go around, and from what I've seen under the sheets, you are no stranger to pain or being a hero. I'm honored to work on you, and I want you to know that I'll do my best to restore your health to something manageable, at least."

He waits until I respond before going any further, and I do. A simple yes is all I can muster.

"With that being said, and without knowing what all Jayden here has filled you in on, let me give you the highlights. When you got shot, the bullet went in through your chest, putting a pretty good sized hole in your lungs. We were able to repair most of the damage when you first came in, but it wasn't your only problem. After passing through your lungs, it hit your spine and caused serious spinal cord injury. As a result of that injury, you are suffering significant paralysis that without attempts to repair will leave you permanently paralyzed from the chest down.

"There is an extreme amount of swelling that we are treating you for that can make some difference in feeling but nothing that will change your prognosis. I must warn you, as weak as you are, the surgery required is extremely risky, and the odds you recover are slight, but for someone as active and deserving as you, we want to give the best chances possible.

"In fact, we have specialists here who have heard what happened and have already volunteered to assist. I recommend you give it a shot, but it's ultimately up to you. I'm going to leave for a few minutes so that you can make your decision, but time is sensitive in this type of surgery. I'll be back shortly."

He offers a courteous smile and just like that, walks out of the room. I just stare at the ceiling. No one braves talking first. I don't know what to feel. I should be comforted knowing they are doing their best. I should feel loved that I'm not alone and others promise to take care of me. I should be relieved that I'm not dead and happy that I saved the one who helped save me, but I'm almost angry. Not that this happened to me, because I know if given the chance to do it all over again, I would do the same but mad because I had plans. I thought we had plans.

I was going to pass on the hope I found by finding someone to give the Bible to, but it looks like there will be no way for me to hand anyone anything. I don't understand why He would allow this vision in my mind of contributing to His kingdom then never allow me to reach the goal. Hot tears form, and I'm mad.

Jayden interrupts my thinking, and I want to scold him as soon as he begins to speak.

"Casey?" he says, but I don't want to listen to anything else right now. The voice in my head is enough. "Casey?" He demands my attention firmly this time, and I comply because he doesn't deserve anything less.

"I know you're upset, but there is more to the story."

When he says this, I stop the runaway train of thinking in my mind and wonder what is important enough that my self-pity can't wait. What else could there possibly be that can trump this particular moment in time that he feels the need to interrupt my mourning prematurely?

I turn my head almost to announce the feelings silenced inside of me, and he leans carefully into me, along with the others. Something seems to be even more secret than how I feel, and as they huddle in around, blocking me from others' view, I can't tell if it's me they are protecting or someone else they are trying to keep out. He continues and I'm curious.

"The guy you just met is a hard skeptic."

He just about whispers this information, and I understand that not believing someone or something can make for dif-

ficulty, but what that has to do with me at this point is not
clear or even relevant. He starts telling me something that I
don't remember.

"When I first met him, it was right after the surgery he
just told you about. He came out to let me know how it went
and what to expect next. He said that at one point you were
semi-conscious after they brought you in, but you were
delusional and not making any sense. He said it was a result
of blood loss and not abnormal for someone to make unclear
suggestions while in that kind of state, but he couldn't get
you to calm down until you made him acknowledge what
you said.

"He told me that you kept saying that everything was
okay because God was in you, and he had to agree before
he could move on or begin working on you. He said he did
for argument's sake, but it's quite obvious he doesn't believe
in God or anything that can make any of this okay."

He pauses for a second, and I assume it's to see if I recall
any of what he just said, but I don't remember this happening at all. I blink twice to let him know that I don't.

"It's okay. He told me that you more than likely wouldn't
remember any of it happening, but it doesn't matter. What
it did do was get me thinking why you were so persistent
with this particular person, so while we were waiting for
you to wake up we did research.

"Casey, sometime before the guy worked here at this hospital, he was stationed on board the USS Carl Vinson, the
nuclear-powered aircraft carrier. Casey, do you understand
where I'm going with this? He qualifies as someone to pass
the Bible on to. There was a reason you were firm with this
guy from the very beginning. We think you found who
we're supposed to pass the Bible on to."

He stops and searches my eyes for recognition and agreement of what he is trying to say. He reads my mind and

brings forth the answer from somewhere behind me. The leather back falls open, and he brings the worn-out book close enough into our circle that I can feel the wind off of it when it joins us.

I can see the command to pass the book on, and God gets on to me for doubting without even having to move from his perch. His plans never changed. I just came to a point where I didn't believe it was possible for me to still carry them out.

I want to cry, but this time it would not be tears of pain and confusion but ones of joy and peace. I look back at the six eyes studying me so intently and have a much different perspective than just moments ago. I can't keep them waiting, nor can I contain the excitement and appreciation of my brothers not quitting on me. I blink once so they know that I'm in mutual agreement with their plan.

As soon as the smiles begin forming on their faces, I tell them exactly how thrilled I really am. I cross my eyes and focus on the innermost part of my nose. Then I blink at least 20 times as fast as I can. I conclude this extravaganza by rolling my eyes as dramatically as possible. Laughter fills the air, and we are all of one mind.

My next question is, of course, the details. Steven speaks up and tells me that he couldn't get anyone to agree with his suggestion of holding the doctor hostage and forcing him to read it. I laugh and almost choke on the ventilator gagging my throat. I can feel a soreness far in the back, and I squeeze my eyes shut to push this discomfort away.

"Hey, you okay?"

I open them at the sound of Jacob worrying, and while I do I catch a glimpse of him lightly elbowing Steven in the stomach as a reprimand for disrupting my comfort. I blink once and reassure him. Jacob proves his age in assaulting a fellow twice his size, and I can see that they are already making friends. I love it.

"But we're not going to do that horrible, very bad, freedom-threatening idea. We figured we would just do what we can in the moment. I think we should give it to him when he comes back for your answer. He believes you should have the surgery so badly that we can probably use that as leverage for him to take it. You'll agree to the procedure if he accepts his challenge. That is, of course, only if you are wanting to follow through and actually do the surgery?"

Jayden offers a very good idea and about the only one I can be present for. I blink. I can't believe this is actually going to happen. I'm almost nervous and now kind of glad that I can't talk. I'm terrible with words and would probably stutter the entire time.

Jayden lifts the Bible higher and centers it above me. He takes my hand and presses it against the outside cover. On top of it, Jayden holds it into place for me. Steven then rests his on top of Jayden's, and of course Jacob lands on the peak of our point.

"Lord, let Your will be done. Amen."

Jayden's prayer is simple yet powerful. The second it concludes, I hear with my super-adjusted ears that our doctor is on his way into the room, and my heart drops with nowhere for it to go.

"Well, I trust that I have given you enough time to make your decision?" he asks. Sticking to our plan, Jayden speaks up for me.

"Doc, Casey here has an interesting proposal for you. He has agreed to do the surgery that you recommend on one certain condition. That you accept this book."

As soon as he says this, the doctor looks confused. Steven and Jacob leave the right side of my bed and surround the middle-aged doctor like you would see hired men do on TV. I'm almost scared of them myself. The atmosphere in the room changes suddenly, and it's noticeable to everyone. This is no joke, and the terms he must agree to are non-negotiable.

"Hey, uh, gentlemen, what's going on here? What are you talking about?" The confident doctor from earlier actually looks nervous.

When Jayden answers him, both Steven and Jacob fold their arms over their chest at the same time and stand firmly, refusing to back down from their position. Jayden goes on.

"Sir, this worn-out book you see here in my hands is no ordinary piece of plain literature. It has a unique history that once it's possessed by someone, has to be maintained at all costs. The instructions on specifically what to read can be found on a handwritten note on the last page.

"Inside, you will also find a flyer that will take you to a place where you will learn what you have to do with this book when you are finished reading. Please realize this is not a joke but a condition. Casey will comply with your offer to help him, if you will agree to his offer to help you."

Jayden beautifully executes a proposal that no decent man could refuse. It's just a Bible, after all, and to an atheist, what harm can a book really do? I expect him to accept, and we will all just have to trust the Lord that He will do the rest. The doctor evaluates the three men standing in front of him and doesn't try to decline our offer.

Instead, he looks to me and asks "Casey, is what these men say true? You will agree to let us try and help you if I agree to take this Bible and follow the written instructions in the back?"

I blink without hesitating and stare deep into his vulnerability. The absence of belief will have God's work cut out for Him, but with no more delay he answers.

"Very well, then. I'll agree to take your book and do what it says." He holds down the nurse's call button by my side, and when they answer he tells them to get Casey Shaw prepped for surgery STAT.

"I can't promise you that we will succeed in fixing you, Casey, but I'll do what you have asked me to do regardless."

I blink once, and he asks my bodyguards to please excuse him if they wouldn't mind. My brothers create a gap and allow him to pass through. After he is completely out of earshot, we all look at each other with amazement written across our faces. Everyone looks awestruck; Jacob speaks first.

"Did he really just accept your terms? I can't believe you got that doctor to agree the way you did. By how you said he spoke earlier, I thought there was no way he was going to take it no matter what we did. Oh my gosh. That's crazy." His hand cups his mouth and of course Steven has something funny to say in response.

"Come on, now, he knew I was going to beat him up if he didn't take it. He's just smart."

"You're so stupid." Jacob tells Steven how he really feels, and we all burst into laughter.

My squinting shows that it's painful for me to join them, and Jacob reprimands Steven for it.

"Don't worry about him, Casey. He's just special. I can already tell."

I blink once to agree with Jacob's comment, and Steven scolds me with no sympathy for my lifeless body. My anxieties from earlier dissolve, and Jayden is the first to speak the truth.

"No, God did it. He orchestrated this whole event all the way down to the flyer that I found on Casey's floorboard."

I wanted to know the details about that when he mentioned it, but I forgot in all of the excitement over the doctor accepting the Bible. I give Jayden my confused face, and he explains.

"When I went to your truck to get the Bible out, as I was opening the door, the flyer fell out. It's how I knew where to send him when he is done reading. It was an ad for that coffee shop that you were supposed to take us to tomorrow."

I rewind in time and search for when I would have picked up a flyer to the café, but such a time does not exist. I never did, and suddenly I remember being the lucky recipient of an unwanted advertisement outside of the Night Bar a couple weeks ago.

I remember the nuisance and recall me enthusiastically tossing it inside of my truck as trash to be thrown out as soon as I got home. It must've fallen somehow and remained out of sight until it was time for it to be rediscovered. My story has a new detail, but I don't get to share it. All I can do is blink. We are interrupted in the middle of our victory and brought back into a sobering reality. We are at the beginning of another fight.

A young nurse walks in and declares, "I'm sorry, but we have to ask you to wrap things up and leave. The anesthesiologist is on his way, and he doesn't like for his concentration to be split by anyone other than the patient."

She stands there as if that can make them obey her. They all turn and face me instead. Jacob is the first to tell me again that he loves me. Steven seconds that fact, and Jayden just stares at me. An avalanche of suppressed emotion escapes from its hiding place, and he is no good at concealing the pain of goodbye.

Moisture saturates the sides of my face, and Jayden is a friend above all I've ever known. I'll never be the same no matter the end result of this surgery, and we both know it. He leans over and rests his cheek against mine.

I can feel the pain in his touch, and I would give anything to wrap my arms around him and console him, but I can't do a thing to comfort my friend. I can't even tell him how many times his hope and his sword have saved me. I weep and our tears mesh. As they do, a longed-for peace comes over me. I'm reminded that Christ is not limited by silence.

He pulls away, and Steven and Jacob are standing by his sides to do what it is that I can't. They place their arms around his shoulders and reassure him. They gradually lead him to the door, where the nurse instructs them where they can find the room that is appropriate to wait in.

I watch them leave until there is nothing left to see. Right as I begin to turn my head back towards the ceiling, I have new company. I don't have time to process anything further before another unknown individual steps up and introduces himself.

"Hello, Casey. My name is Chad." Trapped between the bottom of a green surgical cap and the top of a white surgical mask are a pair of bright, brown eyes that clearly differ from those of Dr. Roy's. I can tell he is smiling as he greets me. I'm interested to see what role he plays in my operation.

"I'll be your anesthesiologist throughout the surgery, making sure that you are properly medicated for pain and remain sedated while the doctors are working on you. It's not my first time, nor will it be my last, so you are in good hands."

He smiles again and his eagerness tells me he has more to say. "I'm sure you have heard this speech once or twice before considering the multitude of scarring, and the x-rays that I have seen of you. I'm honored anytime I get to work on veterans, and in hearing what brings you here today proves what I've been saying for years: Once you're in, you're never really out!"

He changes the subject. "Now I understand that blinking once is your answer for yes and blinking twice is for no. Have I been told correctly, Casey?" He waits, and I oblige with the proper response in order for him to continue.

"Good, good. Now, I'm dying to know, how you did it?"

He pulls down his mask after he asks me the question I clearly can't answer with my limited form of communication, and I wonder why he asks something he knows that I can't respond to. He steps in closer to me, reminding me of the huddle that was just in here.

"Look, while Doctor Roy is out of the room, I just wanted to let you know that however you got him to take that Bible is a real work of God. I've been trying to witness to him for months now, and all he does is brush me off. He's a man of science and numbers. He discredits anything supernatural.

"I'm serious when I say that it's already a miracle that he kept it. I followed him and watched him lock it up in his office myself. I was about to give up on the whole idea of reaching out to him until you came. When I saw him carrying the Bible out of your room, I just knew the Lord sent you.

"I've been praying and praying that if I fail to reach him, that He will send someone who can. What I'm trying to say is that, in a way, I've been expecting you. Casey, Doctor Roy is excellent at what he does, but if he meets the Lord, there is no telling his limitations or the amount of people he can reach.

"Now, I know the statistics of how this all will turn out are stacked against you, but you have to know that you have already overcome insurmountable odds and made a tremendous mark on this Earth. God used you and your experience as a conduit today in order to extend His grace to another, and if nothing else brings you peace in this life, knowing this should."

I discover why he asked for the others to leave. I again am without words to express how I'm feeling, even if the opportunity to share were available. My face rains with affirmation of the Lord's presence, and I'm no longer afraid of what comes next. Chad begins performing his job duties, and my mind drifts to another time and place. My God is forever, and I dream of what that looks like.

CHAPTER TEN

Dear Dan,

This bank envelope is not large enough to write all that I feel. I look around and am in awe at the lives that have been changed because of Christ our Lord. I'm privileged to be among you and honored to be called brother. I see today the accuracy of Scripture that indeed there are many plans in the minds of men. But I now know that the purposes of the Lord will stand.

I want to assure you that I take my responsibility to pass on His words as the most important mission of my life. This, above no other, is a cause worth dying for, and if I were to die today, I would live.

There is no greater comfort in the world than this piece of knowledge assured by God himself. I thank you with all the wholeness of a new heart in Christ.

OORAH,
Sg

AUTHOR BIO

J enny Reese Clark is a living testimony of what true faith in Jesus Christ can bring. As a multiple felon of various drug charges including Unlawful Manufacturing of Methamphetamines, Jenny is no stranger to breaking the rules or suffering their consequences.

In April of 2010, Jenny's life hit an all-time low as she turned her back on the home burning behind her. As a result of a chemical interaction, the clandestine laboratory that she brought secretly into her sister's home exploded. As she took off shoeless, she ran as far as she could to escape the consequences. With her sister's pet dead inside and her re-lationships destroyed through her own betrayals, Jenny woke up as a Jane Doe on a ventilator in an ICU 24 hours later knowing there was no way to come back from such de-struction.

Growing up in a home that offered her as much encour-agement as anyone could ask for, the path she chose didn't equal the opportunity given to her. On March 7th 1999, Jenny was in a serious car accident that left her with plates, screws, and in a wheelchair for months. It was then she discovered the benefits opiates could offer her, and within a few short years, she unintentionally claimed the title of full-blown drug addict.

It wasn't until Jenny went to prison on a 15 year sentence and lost every relationship, possession, and privilege she ever had that she began to honestly understand her true need and dependency upon the Lord. She returned to her roots and picked up her biblical studies where they left off, this time clinging to every word knowing it meant her life or death.

After completing her first Christian fiction novel only a year and a half after her release, in her own words, she shares why she chooses to exploit her past weaknesses before the world.

"I'm not proud of how I've obtained the authority to write or speak on the subjects I do, but my incarceration and faith go hand in hand. Until I was still, I couldn't see past myself; once I surrendered my selfish ways, the haze lifted and life began. The many lessons achieved through a consequence so great, is what inspires me to share these stories that carry both warning and hope."

Jenny's love and dedication to both the Lord and people is clearly evident in her writing and outreach efforts. To learn more about Jenny and her mission to serve others, visit jennyreeseclark.com.